RUN
THE
BLOCKADE

RUN THE
BLOCKADE

★ ★ ★

G. Clifton Wisler

HarperCollins*Publishers*

FOR DONALD

Run the Blockade

Copyright © 2000 by G. Clifton Wisler

All rights reserved. No part of this book may be used or reproduced in any manner whatsoever without written permission except in the case of brief quotations embodied in critical articles and reviews. Printed in the United States of America. For information address HarperCollins Children's Books, a division of HarperCollins Publishers, 1350 Avenue of the Americas, New York, NY 10019, or visit our website at www.harperchildrens.com.

Library of Congress Cataloging-in-Publication Data

Wisler, G. Clifton.

Run the blockade / G. Clifton Wisler.

p. cm.

Summary: During the Civil War, fourteen-year-old Henry finds adventure working as a ship's boy and lookout aboard the "Banshee," a new British ship attempting to get past the Yankee blockade of the Southern coast.

ISBN 0-688-16538-9 (trade) – ISBN 0-06-029208-3 (library)

1. United States–History–Civil War, 1861–1865–Blockades–Juvenile Fiction. [1. United States–History–Civil War, 1861–1865–Blockades–Fiction. 2. Sea stories.] I. Title.

PZ7.W78033 Ru 2000 [Fic]–dc21 99-87298

2   3   4   5   6   7   8   9   10

❖

First Edition

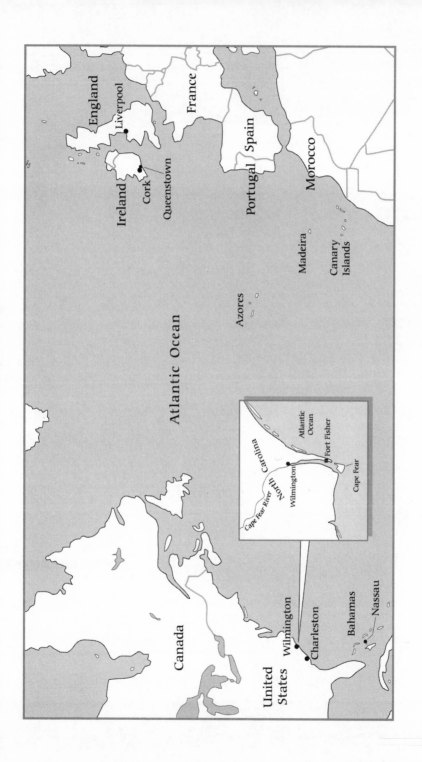

1

THERE IS A RHYTHM to the sea, an ebb and flow that draws a person to its distant mysteries. I felt it the first time my uncle Quin took me to the ocean. I was seven. Off in the distance the waves crashed furiously against the rocky Irish coast. In the protection of the cove of Cork, though, I felt safe.

"You feel it too, don't you, Henry?" my father asked the day I stood at the quay at Cork, waiting for him to join Uncle Quin aboard *Louisa* for yet another journey to the distant shores of America. "Can you sense the power of the waves?"

"I can, Fa," I answered.

"It's the beating of the earth's own heart," he told me. "A man who can feel the tempo of the sea will always belong to it."

"Fa?" I asked, not really understanding.

"The sea calls to some men," he explained. "Those who feel it are never quite at home far from the pounding of the surf."

Of course, there was no surf pounding in the harbor, but I understood just the same. I always had a fondness for the water. I longed to join Fa and Uncle Quin aboard the three-masted barque. I looked enviously at the passengers huddled together on deck, setting out across the Atlantic.

I wished I had spent more time gazing at my father. I never saw him again. Tom Severn drowned off the Massachusetts coast when *Louisa* ran onto the rocks.

Sometimes Mother read the letter the captain had written afterward. It told how Father and Uncle Quin had refused to leave until the passengers got ashore. As a gale ripped the ship apart beneath their feet, they helped two families into a ship's boat. Then they started swimming the others to shore.

It must have been a comfort to the pitiful, frightened children, hugging Fa's back as his strong arms carried them to safety. I remembered clinging to him as he carried me into the ocean before teaching me to swim. Three times he and Uncle Quin swam children to safety before the winds and waves overpowered them on a fourth attempt. The tide brought their battered bodies ashore after the storm subsided, and the townspeople buried them with the six others who never got off *Louisa*'s decks.

"A sailor is bound to ensure the safety of his passengers," Father Andrew, our parish priest, told me later.

Mother rarely spoke ill of anyone, but when I shared the priest's words, she reminded me that the captain and the mates were safe enough, as were the rest of the crew. Only Fa and Uncle Quin had stayed.

"Maybe Fa was thinking of us," I said, remembering our days at the ocean or the times we'd gone swimming in the cove.

"Perhaps," she replied.

But I knew she wished he had considered the plight of a fatherless family left to fend for itself. As for the captain, he sent only the letter. When I later read the whole thing for myself, I saw what Mother had never shared. Captain Dobbins explained that since Fa and Uncle Quin had failed to complete their voyage, they could not be paid.

"Shipwrecked sailors are due something," my sister, Colleen, grumbled. "How is a man to sail home aboard a sunken ship?"

Our misfortune turned to ruin. Friendless and without means of support, we were turned out of the cottage that had been home all my life.

"Come, no tears," Mother scolded us. "We're not the first Irish family turned out by a hardhearted Englishman!"

Her words troubled me some, for Fa was English. I didn't speak the old language, as Mother and Uncle Quin had. I was proud to be named for Fa's father, who had served with Lord Nelson aboard *Victory* as a boy of twelve when the English had wrecked Napoleon's fleet at Trafalgar. Mother was an O'Brien, though. She had often told us our blood was the same blood that had flowed through the veins of Brian Boru, the last king of Ireland. A proud name didn't fill one's belly, though.

It was 1857, a time when plenty of people in Cork remembered the potato blight and the great starving that had followed. We often visited the churchyard where Grandmother and Grandfather O'Brien, together with more aunts, uncles, and cousins than I could remember, lay buried. My baby brother, Christopher, and my stillborn sister, Sarah, were there as well. Two of Mother's sisters and one brother had sailed to America while she and her oldest brother, Quinlan, had remained in Cork.

Now he too was gone.

We passed a desperate month in Cork, living in a garden shed while Mother and Colleen cooked and cleaned for a family named Granger. The little money Fa had saved and the dollars sent us by Mother's sisters in New York didn't last long. My brother Tim and I tried to catch fish to help feed us, but we weren't the only hungry children haunting the river, and bigger boys often took our catch.

My cousin Robert Severn came to the rescue. He was just seventeen at the time, but his father had sent him to school. He had a good job as a shipping clerk in Liverpool, across St. George's Channel in England. Robert arrived just when we were at the end of our rope.

"I'm sorry to have been so long in coming," he apologized the day he arrived. "I didn't know how bad things had become."

Mother avoided his glance. Colleen, as was her habit, stiffened her ten-year-old backbone and planted a hand on each hip. I huddled with my brothers Tim and Francis, gazing at the kind-eyed stranger with more hope than was probably due. We were virtually penniless, with only two boiled potatoes for our dinner.

"I know how hard it would be to leave your home," Robert told Mother, "but I can offer you work with my employer in Liverpool. We have a packet sailing tomorrow, and if you want to come, I can manage passage. My father can send some money if you choose to stay, but that may be weeks in coming. I have a few pounds myself—"

4

Mother cut him off.

"No one in my family is afraid of work," she declared. "I hope to earn enough to buy passage to America."

"You have relations there," Robert said, nodding. "Well, you have one in Liverpool as well, and ships sail every day from there to New York and Boston. Mr. Williams, my employer, is in need of a housekeeper, and he offers you a small cottage and a living allowance. It won't be much money, I'm afraid, but perhaps enough. The children would be welcome at the Cathedral School. Later, when they're older, I might be in a position to offer the boys work."

Robert paused to lift my chin and give Tim and Francis a tap on the shoulder.

"School, you say?" Mother asked.

"Father Devlin comes from Cork himself, and he's promised to tend to it. I won't promise they'll learn more than Latin and numbers, but that's a start."

"It's more than we can hope for here," Mother said. "The answer to a mother's prayer, in fact."

And so we departed Cork and Ireland, my birthplace and home for all my life. It was hardest on Mother, who left not only her past but two buried children in Cork as well. For my brothers, sister, and me, the journey across St. George's Channel and the Irish Sea and then up the River Mersey to Liverpool was our first real adventure. Although the life we found there was far from paradise, we would no longer be hungry.

I don't think Mother ever lost her hope of taking us all to America, but as the years came and went, we grew accustomed to Liverpool. I confess that I often looked longingly at the sailing ships and steam packets moored to the quays, but I wasn't the kind of boy you would expect to have adventures. No, I was the sort you wouldn't spot on a crowded street. And Liverpool streets were nearly always crowded.

By 1861, when the American Civil War began, I was twelve. Liverpool was full of lads my age and size, most of them scurrying about, trying to pick up a few pence selling newspapers or shining shoes. For a time my brother Tim, who had turned eleven, helped me row gentlemen across the river. When summer arrived, we took nine-year-old Francis out in a dinghy and tried to hook a few fish. If we had luck, we attempted to sell our catch along the docks. Most of the time we simply had a bit extra to eat.

Then, in September, Robert found me a regular job at Williams Brothers, the company where he worked as a clerk. Mother had hoped I might continue my education, but Tim was the family scholar.

"We've taught him his letters, Adara," Father Devlin said, using her Christian name for the first time I could recall. "He can read and write, and he actually shows some promise with numbers. His head's in the clouds, though. Perhaps what's needed is the discipline of a job."

I didn't argue, even after Colleen warned me that Mr. Williams was certain to work me hard. "He gets his shilling's worth from everyone," she said. "If I had the chance to lounge about, reading and such, I would take it."

She would have too. At one time I thought Colleen was just being kind, sitting beside the fire and helping Tim and me work through our lessons. Gradually I realized that she was teaching herself in a week what Father

Devlin had to coax out of his classroom of boys in a month! It vexed me to see how hard Mother and Colleen worked, cooking and cleaning for the Williams family. I vowed to ease their burden with the sixpence a week I would earn.

I was probably overpaid. Aside from running down to the docks to check on some ship's repairs or inspect the sailing lists posted by the harbormaster, I was little more than a sweep boy. I kept the floors and windows clean, and I emptied the rubbish tins. It was honest work, but it left far too much time for dreaming. Again and again I felt the pull of the sea.

Then it happened, the event that changed my life forever. On a January morning in 1862 a sleek steam packet appeared out of the Mersey mists flying an odd new flag. It had a circle of seven white stars in the upper corner with two red stripes and one white stripe across the remainder of its length. When I told Robert, he nodded.

"It's the southern Confederacy's flag," he explained. "They've probably sent someone to inspect the ships they're building downriver at Birkenhead."

I had paid little attention to news of the war in America. Mother worried that my uncle Pat would come to harm, for he was still young enough to be a soldier. None of us had concerned ourselves with the southerners. In Liverpool, though, there was a great deal of sympathy for the South.

Living in the largest port of a seafaring nation, shippers and sailors resented the blockade imposed on southern ports. Union gunboats and cruisers stopped any ship they could catch approaching a southern seaport. Many English ships had been captured and their crews imprisoned. Those same warships prevented merchant ships carrying cotton grown in the South from reaching England. Millions of textile workers had also been thrown out of work because of the scarcity of cotton. Queen Victoria issued a proclamation of neutrality, meaning we would not take sides, but English captains running the blockade faced no penalties from English authorities. The soaring price of cotton promised large profits, and the North's blockading ships were far from effective.

"It's perilous work," Robert told me, "but it promises great rewards. Cotton bought for pennies in Charleston, South Carolina, can be sold for a fortune here."

That very week Mr. Williams and his partners called on Robert to organize just such an enterprise. He would arrange the purchase of a ship and sail aboard as supercargo, the representative of the shipper and supervisor of the cargo itself. I looked at the excitement filling his eyes and envied him the work.

"I've found a ship," he told me later. "*Despatch*, a former Irish cattle boat. Older than I'd hoped for, but a steamer. There's a place aboard for a ship's boy if you want to follow your father's trade."

I could have jumped ten feet in the air. All the adventures I had dreamed of seemed to be waiting for me. Moreover, Robert told me that as a crewman I would earn twenty-five pounds for a single voyage. It was more than I could make in twenty years as a sweep boy.

I felt like a starving man who had been offered a crust of bread. It was all I could manage to wait until the office closed. I ran home and charged inside, blurting out my exciting news. Tim and Francis raced over to get the details. "Twenty-five pounds?" Colleen gasped. "Sterling? Are you sure?"

Despite the excitement flooding the room, Mother grew solemn. "It's impossible," she said, frowning.

"Mother?" I asked. "It's not. Robert's made the arrangements himself. I'll be with him."

"No, you won't be," she declared. "I've lost a husband and a brother to the sea. I'll not suffer another loss. It's hard enough knowing Robert's bound to put his life at such risk. For what? So some miller can grow rich? So a southerner can buy and sell other human beings? It's as poor a reason to sell one's life as I can imagine!"

"Mother, I wouldn't be carrying powder for the cannon like Grandfather Severn," I cried.

"Your father wasn't carrying powder," Mother reminded me. "You don't know the sea. You haven't watched it carry away your family. You haven't had to live with the ache of loss as I have."

I winced. I'd lost my father, hadn't I? I had never even seen little Sarah, but I had been old enough to hold Christopher. Colleen and I had washed and dressed him for the funeral! The sea wasn't the only peril to be found.

"Twenty-five pounds," I said. "More if I prove my worth."

"You're worth more than that to me," Mother said, motioning me closer. "I won't have it, Henry. I won't."

There's a time when a boy knows there is no point to arguing. I could see in her eyes the defiance of Brian Boru, the refusal to yield further. I hung my head. She clutched my shoulders and tried to pull me to her side, but I wriggled free. It wasn't that I didn't value my

9

mother's love. I was twelve and a half years old, though, and I didn't intend to pass my life as a sweep boy.

"She has higher hopes for you," Colleen told me that night as we sat together, enjoying the dying warmth of the fire.

"Maybe," I said, "but a sailor's life isn't so bad. Fa died only because the captain and the rest of the crew left. Together they could have saved those people and themselves too."

"Father Devlin says it's all part of God's grand plan," she whispered. "Good may yet come of this."

"Twenty-five pounds," I said, tasting the future it could buy for all of us. "It would pay our passage to New York. You and Mother could work in Aunt Meara's dress shop. All these years of scrubbing floors and emptying chamber pots would be over. And what about Tim and Francis?"

"It's not your job to look after us," Colleen said, resting her chin on my forehead as if to remind me that I was still smaller than she was. "We've put some money aside, you know."

"It won't pay for Tim's schooling," I said, sighing. "It won't be enough either. I've heard you talk about America, about how our cousins go to school there even though they're not wealthy. Colleen, when will we have a better chance than this?"

"Later," she said, brushing rebellious strands of light brown hair from my eyes. "Wait and see if I'm not right." I started to argue, but she put a finger to my lips. "I always am," she added. "Trust me to know."

Perhaps it was true. Mother had grown fond of sharing her old stories of Irish fairies and spirits, and there was something magical in Colleen's eyes that night. Even though Mother refused to allow me to join Robert aboard *Despatch*, his departure left an opening at Williams Brothers. Mr. Franklin Williams, the brother who ran the Liverpool branch of the company, called me into his private office. I was not yet thirteen, and standing in my shoes, I wasn't quite five feet tall. Mr. Williams looked me up and down, from stem to stern, as he called it. He asked me questions, had me write out a letter, and gave me numbers to tally.

"You're far too young to make an adequate clerk," he finally announced. "What have you to say to that?"

"I *am* too young," I said. "But you know my mother and sister. I come from a family of workers. You've seen me sweep a floor. I never got the shipping news wrong, did I? What's the worst thing that can happen if you hire me and I prove unable to do the job? You can always keep my salary and get some exercise by giving me the boot."

He couldn't help laughing at that final suggestion.

"I can see Robert's had an effect on you, Henry," Mr. Williams said. "I had less reason to hire him, and he's never disappointed me. There's not another young man in Liverpool I'd trust half as far. The job will prove tedious, and a week from now you'll probably wish you were still running to the quays three times a day. Nevertheless, I'll pay ten shillings a month if you prove capable. You don't know of a youngster who would care to earn sixpence sweeping out the office, do you?"

"I have a brother," I answered.

"Indeed, you have two," he said, grinning. "I'll probably have them both in my employ before I've finished."

I started to reply, but he hushed me. "Ask your mother if Tim would care to accept the position. I know she has aspirations for the boy, but he wouldn't sweep floors forever. You didn't."

2

THANKFULLY MR. WILLIAMS was right. I didn't remain a clerk long. However, it seemed like forever at the time. While Robert set sail aboard *Despatch* to begin his career as a blockade-runner, I turned to the daily business of recording the goods shipped and received by Williams Brothers. I was one of four clerks and the youngest by a decade, so I rarely got anything interesting to do. Most days I tallied long lines of figures or recorded the departures and arrivals of ships.

The others seldom had a kind word for me. I think they resented me for being so young, but perhaps they simply missed Robert. I quickly learned that everybody had relied on him to do more than his share of the work.

If not for Tim, I think I would have gone crazy. When I grew weary of the work, he would whisper a joke or find an excuse for me to accompany him on some errand. We had always been close, what with only a year separating our birthdays, but at Williams Brothers we became real chums. We were of a kind, people said. Even friends often took one of us for the other. I was a thumb taller, but we both had our mother's light brown hair and blue eyes. I considered myself lucky because Colleen and

Francis had also inherited Mother's Irish freckles. We had our differences, though. While I was usually the one to organize fishing trips or pranks, we both knew Tim was the smart one.

Robert wasn't gone long when Williams Brothers contracted with Jones, Quiggin, and Company for the construction of a new blockade-runner. *Despatch* was proving a poor ship, and this new vessel would be a wonder. It would have a steel hull and be more than two hundred feet long. It being winter and trade a bit slow, Mr. Williams often sent me to the shipyards with messages. Tim could have carried them when he went down to get the shipping reports, but I think Mr. Williams knew I needed the escape. It gave me a chance to watch as the ship took shape.

By February 1863 the ship was more than a steel skeleton. Engineers had installed the engines that would power the great paddle wheels on each side of the hull, and workmen were finishing the odd turtle-shaped deck. I couldn't help pausing to dream of the adventures I might have aboard such a fine ship. Robert's letters and Fa's old stories of life at sea pulled me toward the distant Atlantic.

The day they painted the nameplate, I was there to watch. *Banshee* seemed especially appropriate for a ship that was to race the wind and hide in the mist. Mother's old Irish tales were full of shrieking banshees, female spirits that haunted distant rocky places. Sometimes I felt a similar spirit was hounding me, driving me along to who knew where.

I was a less capable clerk afterward. That was unfortunate because Mr. Williams asked more of me than before. Often he had me recheck the figures of the other clerks.

"I used to rely on Robert for this," he explained. "Now that you're older, perhaps you should have a try."

I accepted my new obligations, but I had little heart for them. For the extra work I was given three shillings each month. The tasks kept me at my desk longer, though, and I made fewer trips to the shipyards.

Tim finally came to my aid by helping check the tallies. He would share my chair, and together we would add the figures. He managed to make a game of it. For me copying out letters and adding figures were a trial that never seemed to end. Tim enjoyed the work and was better than I would ever be at it. Sometimes I looked across the room and saw Mr. King, who must have been a clerk when Fa was wearing short pants. I couldn't imagine spending twenty years doing the same thing day after day!

My impatience grew worse when Robert returned to Liverpool. *Despatch* had been a failure, and he had come home to take charge of *Banshee*. Robert appeared at Williams Brothers in the middle of the afternoon, and we greeted him as a returning hero. He wrapped his left arm around Tim and gripped my hand with his right.

"We must talk," he whispered as he released Tim and greeted the others. After disappearing for a time with Mr. Williams, he returned to my desk.

"Henry, you're to lead the way to the shipyards," Robert explained. "Mr. Williams says you've been keeping an eye on our new ship."

"Well, it's hardly *ours*," I objected.

"That's yet to be settled," he said, motioning me toward the door.

We spent the remainder of the day at Jones, Quiggin, and Company, scurrying about the nearly completed *Banshee*. From his bad experience aboard *Despatch*, Robert had learned a great deal about steamships. He had dozens of questions. I busied myself darting about the vessel, inspecting every fitting and deck plate. The big paddle wheels were particularly fascinating.

When Robert finished his inspection, he practically had to pry me from the ship. I thought he might be annoyed by my interest, but he wasn't.

"Henry," he asked as we walked along the river in the general direction of Mr. Williams's house, "what are your thoughts on going to sea?"

"I dream of it," I confessed, "but Mother won't allow it."

"Even if it was a favor to me?" he asked.

It was a question that hung in the air for several minutes. Then Robert led me to a bench, and we sat together, watching the ships on the Mersey.

"Can I trust you, Henry?" Robert finally asked.

"You know you can."

"I had more trouble at sea than an old ship with bad engines. I grow fretful in my sleep."

"Fretful?" I asked.

"I walk in my sleep," Robert explained. "I did it when I was your age, at school, but I haven't had that problem in years. Then it happened again. It made the crew nervous. Once I slipped and nearly fell overboard. I need someone aboard I can trust to keep me from drowning myself."

"I could do it," I said, "but it won't be easy convincing Mother to let me go."

"Well, if I've learned anything, it's never to be completely certain what will happen," Robert told me. "There are more twists and turns to life than a Liverpool street. We'll give it another try."

Mother was far more predictable than life in general, though. When I brought up Robert's notion, she flatly told me no.

"I won't have it, Henry!" she shouted. "And I've heard all I'll hear on the subject!"

I nodded somberly, but Robert never promised not to speak to her. He had a charm about him that set people at ease, and Mother had long since adopted him as one of her own. At seventeen he had overcome Mother's reluctance to accept help in Cork. Now Robert was twenty-three. Months spent at sea and in the tropics had left him thin but tanned. After sharing tales of his exploits crossing the Atlantic, he suddenly turned somber.

"You seem troubled, Robert," Mother observed.

"I am," he admitted. "You see, it wasn't only the wind and the waves that proved a problem. The sea's a lonely place. I've been on my own since I was eight years old, at school or working for Mr. Williams. Then you came here to Liverpool, and I had a family."

I could see the effect of Robert's words. If they were aimed at Mother's heart, they hit their mark.

"And that's why you want Henry aboard?" she asked.

"Yes," he said. "I also think it's a wonderful chance for a young man to make a future for himself. And his family," Robert added, gazing at Tim and Francis in particular. "Mr. Williams has authorized forty pounds' pay for every member of *Banshee*'s crew."

"It wouldn't be for the money," Mother insisted.

"I understand," Robert said, smiling.

"When we were in need, you offered us a hand," Mother replied. "It's what a family does. I know how hard it is to ask a favor, even when one is owed. It's not often I've had a chance to grant one. Henry, is this truly what you want?"

"Yes, Mother," I said, walking over to her.

"I fear the sea will be lonely for you too," she told me. "It was for your father. Ah, well, I suppose it was bound to be. You'll be fourteen before long. A mother never holds on to her boys forever."

"I'll be back," I promised.

And so it was decided. While *Banshee* completed her fitting out, I was assigned to assist Robert in assembling a cargo and enlisting a crew. Mostly I cataloged bolts of cloth and cases of Enfield rifles. Tim took over my duties at Williams Brothers. And although Francis pleaded with Mother that he should take up Tim's broom, she swept him along to school as before.

The final weeks of February and all of March passed before *Banshee* was ready for sea. Each time the swift little steamer raced along the wharves, townspeople let loose cheers. Here was the first steel ship ever built from the keel up, and anyone associated with the sea recognized that as a milestone. *Banshee* finished out at 220 feet from bow to stern, slightly over 20 feet across, and 10 feet deep. The engineers expected fifteen knots from the twin engines, but they never quite managed that during the trials.

"It's always difficult to predict the results when you're building the first of anything," Robert told me. "I think the engines will pose us some problems. Still, we've got a low-built vessel capable of outrunning anything on the blockade. Compared with *Despatch*, it's a jewel."

Except for the journey from Cork to Liverpool, I had never truly been to sea. I knew nothing of engines and little about sailing. Robert assured me there would be time to learn en route to Nassau, in the Bahama Islands.

As final repairs and modifications were made, I turned to the difficult task of saying my good-byes. I made a final trip to Williams Brothers, but I remained only a few minutes. Tim was copying out bills of lading for us, and the spark in his eye told me everything I needed to know. He was happier than I'd seen him since Fa drowned.

Mr. Williams motioned me into his office, and I sat silently in a chair across the desk from him. He spoke of opportunity and responsibility, but I wasn't paying much attention. When he counted out twenty pounds in five-pound notes, though, my eyes must have grown as wide as saucers.

"Henry, this is half the pay due you for your first trip," he explained. "You give it over to your mother. Once you're in Nassau, making regular runs through the block-ade, I expect you to send at least half your wages home. Robert will manage it for you."

"Yes, sir," I promised.

"See you do as fine a job at sea as you've done here, and no one should have any complaints. Good luck. Make us all rich."

"I'll do my best, sir," I said, shaking his hand. I then pocketed the notes. I half raced home to turn the fortune over to Mother. It was almost as much money as I had seen in my whole life.

I passed the notes into Mother's trembling hands. I

don't think she had imagined coming across so much money at one time. Her eyes grew a little wide.

"I feel as though I've sold my son," she said, hugging me tightly.

"You haven't," I insisted. "It's what I've always wanted, Mother. Fa used to talk to me of the sea, how some men feel it in their soul. That's me. You'll know how best to use the money. I'll send more from Nassau."

"You must write."

"At every opportunity," I said. "I'll tell you everything I see and do."

"We'll expect long letters then," Mother said.

Afterward, when Colleen had completed her duties at the Williams house, I spoke with her as well. She presented me with a warm blue jumper and three pairs of woolen socks. Robert had bought me three pairs of dark trousers and several shirts, explaining that the dark colors would conceal a man from the lookouts of the Union blockaders.

"Will you do something for me?" Colleen asked.

"Anything," I answered.

"Have your likeness taken at the photographer's studio. Henry, you know that Mother worries. Seeing your face will comfort her."

"And you?"

"I'll only have to see Tim," she said, laughing. "And to notice there's less noise."

"I love you too," I told her.

The next day was a busy one, and I returned home late and exhausted. I spent a final night with Tim and Francis in the bed we had shared most of our lives. The room was oddly quiet.

Morning found me rested and excited. After an unusually big breakfast of sausages and eggs, Robert and I prepared to leave. Our sea chests were already aboard *Banshee*, and my new photograph stood proudly on the mantel above the fireplace. Mother and Colleen gave us parting hugs. Francis also wrapped his arms around me. Tim tried to offer only his hand, but he surrendered to his feelings and joined in the melee. I was half squeezed to death, and I don't think Robert got off much easier. I kissed Mother and Colleen farewell and promised for what seemed the twentieth time to write. Then I followed Robert outside.

I had walked the mile to the wharves a hundred times, but it was different that morning. Mists shrouded the narrow streets, and the wind carried an eerie tune.

"*Banshee*'s call," Robert joked.

"Don't jest about spirits," I warned. "Sometimes they know things we don't."

3

ONCE WE REACHED *Banshee,* I found myself introduced to the life of a sailor. First I met the other members of the crew. I had been with Robert when half of them had signed on, but I hadn't paid attention to names. When he brought me before the captain, though, I stiffened and did my best to appear taller.

Captain Jonathon Steele was a trim man with a weathered, wary look. "This the boy?" he asked, studying me.

"My cousin Henry," Robert explained, nudging my hand forward. The captain clamped on to it with a vise-like grip and shook it with enthusiasm.

"No better life for a man than the sea," Captain Steele observed. "Best way to learn the ways of the waters is to get out upon them."

I next met our chief engineer, Mr. Erskine. He was working on the engines at the time and did little more than nod to me. I suspected the last thing on his mind was greeting a ship's boy when he had machinery to manage.

"Don't take it to heart," Robert urged. "Old Erskine's as good as they come. He's been through the blockade and served with the rebels' cruiser *Oreto* early in the war.

Those engines are the heart of *Banshee,* and I judge them in good hands."

Robert next led the way aft to the small cabin we would share. Ordinarily a ship's boy berthed with the ordinary seamen, but Robert wanted me closer at hand. He'd had a hammock slung along one wall for me so that I might keep a weather eye on his nightly wanderings.

After I had satisfied myself that all my belongings were in the small chest he'd acquired for the purpose, Robert led me to the next cabin and introduced me to a tall, thin-faced Carolinian, Tom Burroughs.

"I'm pleased to meet you, Mr. Burroughs," I said, gripping his hand.

"Pleased to meet you, son," he replied, taking a deep pull on his pipe and blowing a circle of smoke toward an open porthole. "It's good to see young, sharp eyes aboard. Where we're going, we're sure to need them."

"Sir?" I asked.

"Mr. Burroughs is our pilot," Robert explained. "He can smell a Yankee cruiser a mile away. Isn't that right, Tom?"

"Oh, from a mile at least," he said, grinning. "And, Henry, call me Tom. I'm no officer. Don't believe half the stories the old men aboard *Banshee* tell, and you'll do well."

I found not a little humor in that as I met the others. There weren't a handful past twenty-five. I wasn't even the youngest. That fate fell to George O'Neal, the other ship's boy.

As we started the dozen-mile journey down the River Mersey past Birkenhead and out into the Irish Sea, I quickly found that George and I were to share every irksome task that befell the crew. To begin with, we were sent to the galley, where a thin-faced young Welshman named Jones set us to work chopping carrots and peeling potatoes.

"See you do it right, youngsters!" he growled. "Else I'll carve you!"

I had spent my share of days helping prepare supper, and I took little offense at such chores. George, who was to turn fourteen in July and thus was younger by three whole months, grumbled the entire time.

"I hoped to be down in the engine room, learning the trade," he told me. "I've been across the Irish Sea to Dublin and back eight times, but never aboard anything like this demon of a ship. *Banshee*'s got no yards on her masts. No sails. I spend two years learning to work aloft, to judge the wind, and here I'm aboard a ship with no sails!"

I tried not to laugh at his exaggerated gestures, but it wasn't possible. He had a heavy Dublin accent, and red hair to boot. At first I wasn't at all sure what to make of George, but we quickly became fast friends. Once we were free of our galley chores, he became my teacher. He showed me how to skin up the mast to the small basket of a lookout post. Then he taught me how to predict the weather by identifying the different kinds of clouds.

"Do you miss home much when you're at sea?" I asked that evening as the sun began to settle into the distant, empty horizon.

"Ships have been my home for so long I can scarce remember any other," he answered. "I was the third of six sons and the fifth of eleven children. My older brothers load cargo on the docks. They won't earn the kind of money I'll make this trip in ten years. I call on Ma and Fa when I'm in Dublin, but they've never found much time for me. My real home's my ship, Henry."

The other sailors seemed to feel the same way. Even Robert took on an affectionate tone when discussing *Banshee*.

"Sailors like to think of their ships as living things," he told me as he helped me climb into my hammock. "They say 'she' or 'her' almost without thinking. I have to learn to do it too, as some take offense to men who do otherwise."

But those first few days it wasn't easy to think of our vessel as a lady!

I had finally managed to adjust to the swaying of the hammock when George appeared at the door, his face full of concern. I tried to step out of my torture contraption of a bed but instead fell flat on my face against the hard steel deck.

"Henry?" Robert cried, blinking himself awake.

"Sir, Mr. Erskine sent me," George said, waving his arms frantically. "We've taken water forward. You'd best have a look!"

To me, taking water meant only one thing. We were sinking! Robert took it a good deal more calmly, but he too seemed concerned. We pulled on our trousers and stumbled out onto the deck. I had trouble steadying myself, and George offered a hand for support.

"Take you awhile to get your sea legs," he explained. "At least you've kept your supper down."

I'd heard enough of Fa's stories of seasick passengers to understand his meaning. I could only hope that was one trial I might escape.

As we made our way down below, following George

to the engine room, I couldn't help noticing the steamy feel of the passageway. Once in the engine room, I saw for myself the cause. The heat generated by two coal-fired boilers was causing the water leaking through the ship's bottom to condense into steam.

"I've started the pumps, Mr. Severn, but we'll never get across the Atlantic this way," Mr. Erskine said, pointing to the inch or so of salt water lapping at the corners of the compartment.

Robert nodded and turned immediately back toward the entry.

"It's *Despatch* all over again," he complained as we made our way along to the cargo hold. Water was seeping in there as well. Fortunately the more vulnerable goods, especially the powder and rifles, were packed highest. Boxes of boots were already wet, but they could best tolerate soaking.

"Will we sink?" I asked.

"No, but we're not going to arrive in Nassau on time," he said, sighing. "More days lost!"

Indeed we learned after sunrise that Captain Steele had already decided to make for Queenstown, as the English called the Cove of Cobh. By afternoon I was spying familiar landmarks along the coast where I had gone with Fa and Uncle Quin years before. My first thought was to find time for a quick visit to my old home at Cork, but I was no idle passenger free to go his own way. Instead, along with the rest of the crew, I worked under Mr. Erskine's direction at bolstering the leaky steel plates. Fortunately there were idle hands at a shipyard to help, for the work was too extensive for us to do alone.

"We'll yet see the Atlantic," Robert promised as the

days passed. "Every child has its teething problems."

Banshee seemed particularly prone to calamity, though, and I found myself sharing George's desire to rig a yard or two in case the engines let us down.

"She'll not support the added weight," Mr. Erskine declared. "For better or worse, we must make do with the engines."

In the end I had time for my visit to Cork, for we were three weeks refitting the plates at Queenstown. It was almost April by then, and a twelve-mile walk was like a treat for my shipbound legs. Years of walking to and from the Liverpool quays had accustomed my muscles to such labor. George, who insisted on going along as a "son of Erin" and my protector from trouble, found the journey more tiring. As for shielding his *English* friend from the locals, George found that his Dublin accent marked him as more of a stranger than my Liverpool snarl, as Colleen called it. I easily slipped back to the old fashion of speaking I'd acquired in my first eight years of life.

I also wrote my first letter home from Queenstown. I hoped it would warm Mother's heart to hear of my trip to Cork. The town appeared much changed. The quays were nearly empty, and the wide streets I remembered seemed as narrow and winding as any I'd known in Liverpool. Mostly I wrote of going to the churchyard. I'd placed flowers on the stone that marked the burial place of my little brother and sister. I couldn't recall the other places, where my grandparents and various O'Brien aunts, uncles, and cousins rested. I was glad to offer some remembrance to little Christopher and Sarah, though.

Once Mr. Erskine and Captain Steele were satisfied with *Banshee's* repairs, we again set out to sea. Spring was far from the worst time to make an Atlantic crossing, but our bad luck held. A gale blew in from the southwest, and it was all Captain Steele could manage to keep us off the rocks at Fastnet. Winds lashed us from three directions at once, and it was more than perilous to attempt one step on deck. Every loose fitting on the ship broke free, and I wondered if the masts themselves might go as well. The forward stokers' compartment flooded, settling us dangerously low in the water. Reluctantly we turned back to Queenstown yet again.

This time, however, the repairs proved minor, and we were back out in the Atlantic that same week. Captain Steele kept us on a southerly course, close enough to the French Biscay ports that we might slip in for additional repairs if necessary. This too had its hazards, though. A ship built for avoiding lookouts can prove a hazard in well-traveled waters, and we were nearly run down by a lumbering French barque. Our engines and Captain Steele's alert handling saved us. Still, we were close enough to hear the jeers of the French sailors and a curse or two as well.

"And this is supposed to be the safe part of the trip," Robert remarked. "The real danger's still ahead."

I learned as much from Captain Steele. Among my duties was serving Robert and the ship's officers in the small dining room they shared next to the galley. Sometimes Captain Steele would recount his earlier exploits. Other days Tom Burroughs would talk about the hazards of slipping through the ring of Union ships surrounding Charleston and Wilmington, the two

Carolina ports favored by Nassau blockade-runners.

"It's a game of cat and mouse," the captain explained, "and it's grown deadlier. More than twenty craft were snagged last month."

"What happens when you're captured?" I asked.

Robert frowned, and I suspected I had violated some shipboard law by speaking. I backed away, trying my best to blend into the bulkhead, but Captain Steele simply laughed.

"How's a boy to learn if he doesn't ask?" the captain said, motioning me to his side. "Henry, you may think you've signed aboard a poor ship, what with the troubles we've had. My first ship, *Tubal Cain*, made its initial run last July. We were still a hundred miles from Charleston when spotted by a Union steamer. If we'd seen them earlier, we might have evaded the enemy. As it was, we eluded them for close to six hours. They fired a shot from a hundred-pounder smoothbore that whined past our bow, and we heaved to. At least we had the comfort of knowing two other runners that were nearby got away.

"*Tubal Cain* carried sails, and to conserve coal, we had only one boiler fired when we were discovered. We were up against an able enemy too. Our pursuer was a new side-wheel steamer out of New York, *Octorara*, commanded by the very Commander Porter who's made himself famous and advanced to the rank of admiral capturing forts on the Mississippi River. I'm sorry to have aided his career."

Robert laughed at the remark, but the others found little humor in the tale.

"There's not an inch of ocean safe for a blockade-runner," Captain Steele pointed out. "The United States consuls send dispatches about each new ship launched at Liverpool, and they have spies in Nassau who do the same thing. Porter told me as much. There we were, a hundred miles off the American shore with bills of lading for our cargo. We might well have been bound for Canada, as our papers said, but the Yanks barely bothered with such matters. It didn't take much pressing before some of the crew gave us up. And so I was sent to New York to enjoy the hospitality of the United States Navy."

"They're not all that hospitable," Mr. Erskine said, fingering his teacup.

Captain Steele grinned and nodded.

"Fortunately the British consul arranged a bond and secured my release," the captain said. "But no sailor ever takes to the confinement of a jail, even it's for a few weeks!"

"Many a good pilot's gone the same way," Tom Burroughs added. "Except, being a Carolinian, I'll have no consul helping me out of my confinement."

I later learned pilots were neither pardoned nor exchanged, for their value to the runners was deemed a threat to the United States. Tom, being especially skilled, was particularly wanted. In return he earned three thousand American dollars, six hundred pounds sterling, for every trip he made! It was a fortune by anyone's reckoning, though it brought considerable peril with it.

I expected us to have a peaceful voyage to Nassau, but nothing could be further from the truth. Off Madeira, while I was manning the lookout post for only the second time, I spied a wisp of smoke on the horizon. It seemed odd at first, for rather than running east or west, as a trading vessel would, it seemed to be bearing south, across the shipping lanes.

"Smoke!" I shouted below.

There were only two crewmen on deck at the time, Keith Davis and John Bailey, but they responded immediately. Davis headed for the steering bridge while Bailey climbed the mast to lend his eyes and experience.

"You did well, lad," he told me as he crowded in alongside me. "She's a warship, most likely a Yankee cruiser."

It was difficult to tell whether the cruiser had seen us or not. We were low in the water and burning good coal. Still, the smoke was growing closer and darker.

"She's putting on steam," Bailey told me. "Best we do the same."

Captain Steele must have thought likewise, for he swung the helm over and drove us southwestward, away from danger. I sighed with relief when I saw the other ship continue along her course. She hadn't seen us after all.

"You've earned your pay today," Captain Steele told me after we had put the cruiser behind us.

It was a little worrisome, seeing ships of the northern navy so far from their home waters. After all, the Americans had always been the loudest champions of the freedom of the seas. Still, what better way to catch a blockade-runner than when she was off her guard, sailing in open ocean?

"It's a bad sign, though," Robert declared. "If they've got cruisers to spare for patrolling the Atlantic, they're bound to have more than ever on patrol off the southern ports."

I nodded. The danger, then, was as great as Mother feared. But I was still only thirteen, and I couldn't imagine *Banshee*'s falling prey to any ship afloat. With Captain Steele at the helm and Mr. Erskine coaxing every ounce of steam from our engines, we were swift and elusive. I considered it a good combination.

Captain Steele valued my eyes, and I found myself assigned the dangerous watches at dawn and dusk, when smoke was difficult to spot. Other times he took me into the chart room and showed me how he marked out our course. By the time we were halfway across the Atlantic, he trusted me enough to allow me to steer the ship.

"You've got a good feel for *Banshee*," the captain told me. "Most men turn the wheel too much, but you leave her be. You trust her to run straight. A man who jiggles the rudder just wastes coal."

"My father used to talk about the tempo of the sea," I said. "Of course, it was different with sailing ships, I suppose."

"Different indeed," Captain Steele agreed. "Better in most ways. But there's no thought of running through a blockade with sails. The wind dies, and you're caught. You need the speed to dart and dodge the enemy's guns."

"Will there be much of that?" I asked.

"It takes only one well-aimed shot to lay us low, Henry. A runner dare not fire in his own defense. That makes him a pirate. No, he has only his wits, the speed of his engines, and the craft of his pilot to get him safely through. And, of course, the eyes of his lookouts."

4

OUR VOYAGE TO Nassau made history. *Banshee* was the first steel vessel ever to cross the Atlantic. For me the trip had been a school. I learned something new every day! It was difficult to remember that I had come aboard to keep Robert from wandering off in his sleep and falling overboard. He didn't leave his berth a single night from the day we departed Liverpool to the day we anchored in Nassau Harbor.

Being a British ship docking in an empire port, we had few problems with customs officials and the like. We secured a berth from the harbormaster, and Robert set about the task of securing fresh provisions for the crew. It was only when I fetched a newspaper that I realized the date—April 20, 1863. I had turned fourteen the day before without realizing it!

To mark the event, Robert insisted I accompany him into Nassau. After we enjoyed a feast of spicy Spanish dishes and fresh fruit, he led the way through town. His obligations to the ship and crew took the first hour or so, but soon enough we were on our own.

"Once this was the greatest den of pirates the world has ever seen," Robert told me as we passed a line of street vendors. "Then, for a time, the old buccaneers settled into a quieter life of mending sails or making barrels. The American blockade has reawakened the old blood, though. Of the three thousand people who live here, there are very few not prepared to pick your pocket or sell you a treasure map to some sunken Spanish galleon."

Saloons and gaming houses lined the waterfront, and I spotted all sorts of tattoo houses. Lively music flooded the streets, and women with every color imaginable painted across their faces waved scarves at us.

"I wouldn't write your mother about everything," Robert urged as I gazed wide-eyed at one of the painted ladies. "She needn't know about some things."

One of the things Mother had reminded me about was the need to visit a church and take communion, but churches were few and far between in Nassau. Robert finally located a Spanish church where a priest celebrated mass and heard my confession. Afterward he gave me a small silver cross and smiled.

"You haven't been in Nassau long, have you?" he asked.

"No, Father," I answered.

"I can always tell," he said, resting his hand on my shoulder. "You didn't have nearly enough to confess."

Nassau was full of lures that could take a sailor's money and even his life. A French sailor was stabbed the second day we were there. Unless I was with Robert, I remained aboard ship. I had no pocket money, and that fact alone kept me away from real trouble.

Aside from finding distractions in town, the crew had work to do in Nassau. Mr. Erskine continued to tinker with the engines while the rest of us undertook the task of preparing the ship for her career as a blockade-runner. At Tom's urging, we removed every unneeded fitting above decks. Less weight meant more speed, and any odd noise could alert the enemy. Mr. Erskine wandered about, listening for just such sounds. He detected them, and we tightened hatches and removed brackets.

Most of our time was occupied with painting *Banshee* dull white. It seemed odd to me, for a light object was sure to stand out against the dark of night.

"Only in moonlight," Tom told me. "The thing that gives you away is the sea turned over by the paddle wheels. Off the Carolinas you'll always have storms about to generate a degree of foam and froth. A lookout searches for a patch that stands out, a dark shape set against the whitecaps."

I also learned that all my efforts to obtain dark clothing had been wasted. My warm wool jumper knitted by Colleen would remain in my chest. At sea we wore only light clothing, and fearfully little of that! George had taught me the value of walking the deck barefooted, but the growing heat of late spring led me to discard my good, durable Liverpool trousers for a pair of knee britches. I don't think one Nassau sailor in fifty wore a shirt. Although I felt a little odd showing off my pale, pitifully frail chest and shoulders, George convinced me to do so. Long hours of painting and loading additional cargo hardened and tanned me. I began to grow taller too.

"It's the salt air," Robert declared when we updated the cargo manifest. "Life at sea suits you, Henry."

"Nobody stays a shrimp all his life," I replied. "Except maybe a shrimp."

The next morning, as we finished preparing for our first run, I noticed we had a number of visitors. One was an attractive girl about my age. She wore a sky blue dress that matched her eyes and a large yellow hat. I couldn't help noticing those blazing eyes. They seemed to burn through me like a pair of comets.

"She's watching you, Henry," George whispered. "She's probably taken with your manly body."

The others likewise cackled at the girl's obvious pre-occupation with my movements. I tried to ignore her, but the longer she stayed, the odder I felt.

"Go over and see what she wants," George urged.

"Best do it, Henry," Tom added. "Take care with what you say, though. The Yanks have spies everywhere."

I nodded. One of the odd things about Nassau was the mix of sailors in the port. Aside from the Europeans, there were many Caribbean and South American seamen. The crew of one of Her Majesty's frigates mixed with a hundred or so sailors from a United States block-ader. As for spies, half the nations in the Western Hemisphere had consuls or agents in Nassau. If there was a particle of information to be bought or sold, Nassau was the market for the transaction.

I strode across the plank to the wharf and smiled at our visitor. "Can I help you find someone?" I asked.

"No," she said, dipping her head shyly. "I just wanted to have a look at *Banshee*. She's all steel, I understand. And fast. How many knots can you manage?"

I started to answer when something gnawing at my insides stopped the words.

"I'm sorry," I said. "I neglected to introduce myself. I'm Henry Severn. And you are?"

"Andrea Fornier," she said, grinning. "My uncle is in the shipping business. Do you carry cargo for Charleston?"

"Do you know Charleston?" I asked.

"I was there before the war started," she explained. "My father's business has taken him many places."

"Is he also in the shipping trade?"

"Oh, no, he builds engines," she said, wiping her brow with a kerchief. "Oh, I'm no good at this, Henry. Here I am, trying to find my way aboard your ship, and you're asking all the questions."

"What exactly aren't you good at?" I asked, growing alarmed.

"Well, you've probably guessed. My uncle's the U.S. consul here in Nassau. He sent me out to have a look at your ship. My brother, Lawrence, would have come, but I can't imagine you'd let him aboard. He's a midshipman in the navy!"

"I don't think I could get a worm aboard," I said, shaking my head. "The captain's shy of visitors most days."

"And spies all the time?" Andrea asked. "Thought so," she added when I nodded. "Well, the navy will have to get by on its own, Henry. If you manage to keep from getting sunk or captured, maybe you'll come by for a visit when you return."

She handed me a small white card with her name neatly printed above the address of a Nassau residence.

"When I return from where?" I asked.

"Why, from running the blockade," she said, laughing. "Dear, you're either very good at this or extremely inexperienced. Everyone knows we're coming to a moonless week. Every runner in Nassau will be off tonight or tomorrow. I won't wish you luck, Henry, but I will say a prayer for your safety. Perhaps if you don't get through, I may visit you when I return to New York in December. There are quite a lot of blockade-runners' crews confined in the harbor forts."

"A cheering thought," I told her.

"Actually it is," she said, smiling wickedly. "We shall get all of you eventually, Henry. A swift ship may run from Nassau to the Carolinas a time or two, but it won't cheat fate forever."

After Andrea strolled away, ignoring the waves and shouts of the crew of a steam packet in the next berth, I returned to my ship and shared the gist of Andrea's conversation.

"It's mostly true, of course," Captain Steele remarked. "The odds are growing in their favor. Still, we're not without a trick or two."

I was soon to learn from my own experience just how sly and elusive Captain Steele and *Banshee* could be. As Andrea had predicted, the little fleet of blockade-runners began slipping out of Nassau in twos and threes. The United States steamer was bound by Crown regulations to delay its own departure a day or so, but several of the crew hired a sailboat and alerted a second Yankee ship to the sailings. When we left the harbor, we spied the enemy vessel waiting just outside the territorial waters.

"Time to see what she can do," the captain announced. And so we began our first run to Wilmington.

A swift ship like our own could travel the 640 miles to the North Carolina coast in three days, but speed wasn't our sole advantage. Low built and burning good coal, we were virtually invisible from any distance at all, and the wisp of smoke we produced could easily be mistaken for a bit of cloud. The larger warships of the United States fleet, on the other hand, tended to produce clouds of dark smoke from their high stacks, and their masts made them visible to a pair of sharp eyes from several miles away. Knowing the general speed and direction of the enemy ship, Captain Steele chose a course that led south and east, away from Wilmington. The Yanks could chase us and leave their advantageous position opposite Nassau Harbor or leave us alone. As Captain Steele expected, the Union warship remained on station and allowed us to escape.

"It's the sensible thing to do," Robert told me once the enemy vessel was out of sight. "They know we can outrun them. Only sensible to wait for a better chance. Of course, if they'd known our engines, they likely would have come on."

I tried to laugh, but Robert's face was serious. For the first time since I'd known him, he was restless and fearful. When I fell out of my hammock that night, he yelled at me.

"When are you ever going to learn how to do that properly?" he shouted. "Your mother may have been right. You'll never make a sailor."

I stared at him with hurt eyes. The words stung. I cautiously spread the side of the hammock out and crawled in. The ship lurched, throwing me back onto the deck.

I expected him to scream again, but instead he helped me up. His face was red, but it wasn't from anger. He was laughing!

"It isn't that easy," I told him.

"Sorry I yelled, Henry," he said, gripping my shoulders. "It's not you."

"I'm a little scared myself," I confessed.

"You're not responsible for thousands of pounds' worth of cargo and a ship and crew," he explained. "It's hard not to be anxious."

"I suppose. I have only my life to worry about, and that's not near so much."

"Henry, I didn't mean—"

Now it was my turn to laugh, and I did just that.

"What's the worst the Yanks will do to us?" I asked.

"Well, they can't very well eat us," Robert said, shaking his head. "But they'll likely do most everything else they can."

"You're not Irish, Robert, or you'd realize how difficult it is to catch a banshee. She's just air, you know. No ship's going to trouble us."

I found myself believing those words. Just the same, I took to wearing my silver cross, and I said my prayers more regularly. George, having grown up around sailors and stevedores, was a bit prone to swearing, and he'd declined my invitation to attend mass at the Spanish church. Just the same he crossed himself regularly and spoke a few prayers as the moon finally passed from the nighttime sky.

Our game of cat and mouse went well following our brief encounter with the Union steamer off Nassau. For two days we saw only another blockade-runner or two. At Tom's suggestion, we approached Wilmington from north of the mouth of the Cape Fear River, where the blockading ships patrolled. In this way we could follow the strong southerly current past the Confederate batteries at Fort Fisher and work our way across the bar at New Inlet. According to Tom, the Union ships were spread thin farther north. Only shallow-draft craft like *Banshee* could run the coastal waters. Moreover, if we got into trouble, the big guns of Fort Fisher could come to our aid.

That first journey to Wilmington was like a second day of school for me. Although we actually faced no peril during most of the voyage, we never had a moment free of potential hazard. Lookouts were doubled, and I slept only four hours at a time. The next four hours I was assigned duty at the lookout post high up on the crosstie of the foremast. Using a telescope at times, but primarily relying on my own eyes, I scanned the ocean for any trace of smoke.

As we approached the treacherous Carolina coastal waters, we entered the first line of outer cruisers. It was these smaller, swift craft that had captured Captain Steele and *Tubal Cain* less than a year earlier. The waters were rough, and we failed to encounter trouble from that first line of blockaders.

The second line was closer to the coast. Most of these ships were powerful gunboats, and their crews were ever alert for any opportunity to take a prize. Some of the gunboats were themselves former blockade-runners, so a lookout could not relax even when spying a familiar ship. Days before, such a ship might have been a sister blockade-runner. With a big hundred-pounder smoothbore cannon on deck, she posed a grave peril.

I was on station in the crow's nest when *Banshee* slithered through the line of gunboats. I saw two of them, but both rode easily at anchor, and only one had any steam up. There was a heavy fog shrouding everything, and I thought that the greatest danger might be striking one of the Yankee ships in the dark. They appeared to be that thick! Actually, though, there was an interval of better than a mile between the two gunboats, and we easily worked our way between them.

Last remained the shallow-draft ships of the inshore squadron. Because they could chase their enemies to the bar, the shallowest point of the channel, they posed a number of problems. *Banshee,* fully loaded as she was, could not cross the bar at low tide, so we would be vulnerable if we grounded on the bottom for even half an hour. The inshore vessels, though, faced the hazards of Fort Fisher's powerful batteries as well as Confederate infantry stationed along the river to prevent invasion.

As we worked our way through the darkness, I felt my flesh attacked by giant mosquitoes. Darkness surrounded us, but the air was calm, and we could hear sounds from miles away. With the ship quieted except for the engines and not so much as the flicker of a pipe showing above decks, we inched our way along the coast. The engine hatches were covered, and the stokers shoveling coal must have suffered terribly from the heat. Eerie as it was on lookout, at least I could breathe.

Tom paced the deck uneasily. From time to time he ordered a line cast overboard to check the bottom. It seemed at times as if he were a blind man groping his way along a busy street. In fact he knew the coast so well he could identify our position by the nature of the sand brought up by the casting.

Gradually we reached a point where I could recognize the faint outline of the coast. I took some comfort from the realization that no enemy craft stood between us and the safety of dry land. A half hour later, though, I caught sight of a phantom on our starboard bow. Any ship between the bar and us posed a problem. Before I could pass the word, however, Tom had altered course to avoid the enemy vessel.

As if one weren't enough trouble, we spied a second gunboat on our left, port side. I was the first to see this one, and I alerted the captain. This enemy too failed to spot us. As we slipped away in a low mist, we suddenly found ourselves confronting a third Union ship. This time I never had a chance to announce my sighting. Captain Steele swung the wheel over, and we avoided collision at the last minute. I heard shouting and cursing from the other vessel, but no cannon fired. They must have mistaken us for a friend.

We began slowing, and the engines grew quieter. I could hear other ships in the distance, but the shoreline had grown into a blur, and I could no longer identify our position. For a brief time Tom also seemed confused. Then a long, rounded hill arose from the mists, and our pilot barked orders. The engines resumed their thunderous tempo, and we headed toward a break in the rocks up ahead. On our right Fort Fisher appeared in the predawn light. It was merely a long line of earthworks, raised mounds of sand, but deadly guns placed there awaited any Union gunboat too reckless to notice. Except for another blockade-runner up ahead, we were the only ship in sight. We headed for the bar.

Daylight was coming upon us, and the gunboats of the inshore squadron could finally see us. Three put on steam and made a run toward us. One fired a single shot that fell short. Even so, the noise and the huge column of water thrown up shook me from head to toe.

We were now in a true sea chase. Three of the enemy gunboats were in pursuit while two others moved off north and south to prevent flight. George shouted out a sounding that warned of shallow water, and we all knew that if we were too deep in the water to make it across the bar, we were certain to be blasted apart. Except for the engine crew, all hands were on deck, and even the hardest sailor among them whispered the words of some half-remembered prayer.

Suddenly cannon fire erupted from Fort Fisher. Big guns boomed out their answer to the Yankee gunboats, and the water erupted near the closest vessel. A second gunboat shuddered from a near miss, and then dark smoke rose from the stern of the nearest boat. The gunboats lost their enthusiasm for the chase, and they turned back toward the Atlantic Ocean. We passed over the bar and continued up the Cape Fear River to safety.

5

OUR FIRST TASK upon passing safely through the Union fleet was to secure a local pilot for the short passage up the Cape Fear River to Wilmington. That seemed odd to me, considering how well Tom knew the Carolina coast. I soon learned the reason. To prevent invasion, Confederate authorities had placed explosive devices called torpedoes at various points in the river. Some lay on the bottom and could be fired off electrically from shore. Others had contact detonation devices and would sink friend and foe alike. The local pilots had maps of the torpedoes' locations and kept us from harm.

Our guide was a tall, thin-faced man nearly fifty years old named Jim Shaw. Too old for the army, he was quick to point out that he had two sons and eight grandsons in the rebel ranks. "The youngest is only fourteen," he boasted. "Serves a gun at Fort Fisher."

It was interesting to listen as old Jim, as he liked to be called, jabbered away in his slow southern drawl with Tom. Between their odd words and Jim's habit of speaking through a mouthful of chewing tobacco, I could make out only bits and pieces of the conversation. I also learned that remaining near anyone chewing tobacco can be as perilous as running the blockade. Jim spattered the deck with brownish liquid every few minutes. If George hadn't yanked me clear, I might have received a good bit of it!

From listening to Tom and others, I had the impression that the South would be a land of tall trees, big houses, and wide avenues. I expected a country of gentlemen planters and beautiful ladies, a land full of marvels. Tom spoke of the easy pace at which southerners walked and did business. I thought, Well, here would be a place to relax and catch our breath.

As we neared Wilmington, I caught only a glimpse or two of large houses. The country was green, but except for occasional parties of soldiers or a group of small boys fishing off the bank, I saw little of the anticipated southern grandeur.

Before docking at Wilmington, we were inspected by a medical officer. It seemed that yellow fever had hit the city hard, killing hundreds of people, and any ship hoping to tie up there had to secure a certificate of good health. The doctor lined us up on deck and looked each of us over and found no sign of sickness. I confess I felt a little like a horse undergoing inspection by a prospective buyer. The doctor poked and prodded much more than I considered necessary. Worse, the rest of the crew seemed to enjoy my displeasure. When we were finally allowed to proceed into port, I breathed a sigh of relief.

"I've seen less fuss made over a June bride," George said, laughing as the rebel doctor slipped on a patch of old Jim's tobacco juice.

"Well, I only recall seeing one other doctor in my whole life," I said, frowning. "He did my little brother no good at all."

"Must have been English," George grumbled, flashing his Dublin grin.

After Robert had rowed ashore to speak with the harbormaster, we were finally allowed to join the line of blockade-runners tied up at the Wilmington wharves. I then had my first good look at the port. It proved to be a real disappointment.

War might have changed things, of course, but our arrival that spring of 1863 found a port city of six thousand people, most of them frantically running about on one errand or another. Yellow fever, old Jim explained, had broken the spirit of the place. Most of the survivors had left for one reason or another. The men had marched off to war. Many of their families appeared to have gone to stay with relations. The Wilmington I saw was a town of foreign sailors, armed soldiers, and gangs of slaves put to work loading and unloading ships. Not far from the wharves stood streets full of gambling parlors and saloons. George and I were inclined toward exploring the place, but Captain Steele was blunt.

"Boys, this is as mean a place as you'll find on earth," he declared. "You stay aboard, the both of you."

Robert echoed the captain's sentiments. "There's no time anyway," he added. "We've got to get our cargo ashore, reload, and be off again before the moon's back."

Mr. Erskine and the engineering crew went ashore, though, as did almost everybody else. Even George slipped off with Tom Burroughs one afternoon. I had hoped Robert would at least let me visit the other blockade-runners tied up nearby, but he insisted I stay in our cabin.

"If you have the time to do something, write your

mother," he scolded. "She'll be wondering about all those letters you promised."

That was true enough. So while the others drifted ashore in pairs, I sat on the deck with my back to the steering cabin, writing my lines as *Banshee* rocked gently to the tempo of the Cape Fear River. I started to write of our adventure breaking through the line of Yankee warships, but I knew Mother would only worry. Instead I wrote of the fine friends I was making, of how my sharp eyes had won the favor of Captain Steele, and of the peace my soul seemed to find on the ocean.

I suppose it's true that I'm Fa's son, I wrote her. *While the others grow dizzy and sick in a heavy sea, I feel at home.*

We were in Wilmington only a short while, but *Banshee* won many friends among the townspeople. While Tom Power, the shipping agent hired by Williams Brothers, arranged for the unloading of our cargo by two dozen black men, Captain Steele let it be known that we would welcome aboard any and all Confederate officials.

Our steel construction being a novelty, we had a swarm of visitors. When the lunch bell rang, our cook, Bob Jones, appeared with platters of stewed beef and salted herring for our guests. *Banshee* boasted bottled beer and brandy too, although I never tasted a drop of either. Before long we found ourselves hosting every sort of port officer and dozens of other Wilmington citizens, invited or otherwise. I particularly remember Miss Carmen French, a famous local entertainer, whose face had more paint on it than *Banshee*'s entire deck.

"You must do something about your appearance, Henry," Robert scolded me after two young rebels had laughed at my bare feet. "What's suitable for duty at sea won't do here. We represent our company and our nation."

So I squeezed my growing feet into a pair of polished shoes, slipped Colleen's jumper over my white cotton shirt, and had Bob clip my hair to a respectable length.

Now that I was presentable, I became *Banshee*'s official guide. Although most visitors were more interested in biscuits and herring, I had the pleasure of escorting a pretty fourteen-year-old girl named Myra Littrell and her brother, Christopher, on a thorough inspection of our ship. They appeared dressed for an evening ball rather than a tour of a steamship. Myra wore a bright yellow dress with a hoopskirt that took up every inch of the passageway. Her brother wore a Confederate military cadet's uniform.

"Does she boast of much speed?" Myra asked when we finally maneuvered her and her skirt to the engine room.

"Not so much as we'd like," I answered. "When a Yankee cruiser is on your bow, you can use every knot the engines can manage."

"Our father's in France," Myra said. "He's trying to purchase two ships for the Confederate navy. If he's successful, the Yankees will have more serious worries than stopping a few little ships from entering Wilmington."

I wasn't entirely pleased to hear her dismiss the blockade-runners so lightly. As for our number, there were more than twenty in port that very day!

"Mustn't worry yourself over what Myra says," Christopher told me afterward. "She likes you. I think she's trying to impress you. She certainly wouldn't drag her best dress through an engine room for anyone else in Wilmington!"

I hoped she might return and stay a little longer. George was good company, but I found myself oddly warmed by Myra's attentions. She didn't reappear, though.

While our hospitality took a toll on our provisions, it did our hearts much good. The army's needs drew most of the food and clothing available on the Carolina coast, and everything was scarce in Wilmington. Word spread, and we often welcomed aboard poor, thin-faced boys and girls who put me in mind of the children Tim and I had fought back in Cork over the possession of a trout. Most eagerly accepted whatever was offered, but two boys about my age remained ashore, sitting on barrels near the wharf. Although they looked longingly at the food George and I carried up from the galley, they made no move toward the gangplank. Wearing tattered shirts and ragged trousers, they nevertheless refused to beg. I sometimes spied them running errands or holding horses, but they rarely received much payment for their efforts. Their hungry eyes haunted me, and I finally urged George to bring them aboard.

"I can't go myself," I pointed out, "but nobody's ordered you to stay aboard."

"Only Captain Steele," George said. I could tell from the glint in his eyes he would do it, though, and the next morning he led our two pitiful guests aboard.

"I'm Francis Marion Hunter," the taller of the two said, making a little bow. "This is my cousin Martin Cloud. I'm afraid we've fallen on ill times."

From their speech you would have mistaken them for two of the Littrells' schoolmates.

"It's early for lunch, but we have some bread," I said,

quartering the half loaf George and I had liberated from the galley.

The boys took their shares and ate hurriedly. I was hungry myself, but I ate only a bit of mine before passing the remainder to Francis. George had already presented his share to Martin.

"I can't," Francis said, handing the bread back to me.

"I have a brother named Francis," I explained, declining it. "And I've been hungry."

"You're a long way from growing fat now," Francis said, accepting the bread.

They gobbled the bread in a manner of minutes, and George found a few sardines for them.

"It's a feast," Francis told me afterward. "Most days we're lucky if we can manage a square of corn bread and some bacon."

"Don't you have any family?" I asked.

"My brother's with the army, in Virginia," Martin explained. "He scarcely has enough to eat himself, and he's rarely paid. Before long we'll be old enough for the army ourselves. Until then we'll find something to do."

"Isn't there work?" George asked.

"For sailors maybe," Francis said, frowning. "Most of the real labor's done by slaves. The government pays their owners."

From all I had read before the war, I expected the slaves to be angry and resentful. Colleen had shared one of Mrs. Williams's books about a pitiful slave girl who had run away, only to drown crossing the river that would have led to freedom. At Wilmington the slaves loading and unloading ships sang and laughed. It was just an illusion, though.

"I suppose Wilmington must be a holiday for them," Martin said, sighing. "Francis and I tried to hire ourselves to a farmer, but the work broke us down, and he never paid us anything. I don't think slaves enjoy themselves much. Thousands have run off to the Yankees in Virginia and down in South Carolina, where the Yanks have landed an army."

"The war's going badly then?" I asked.

"Not for everyone," Martin said, glancing ashore at the shipping offices. "We've done well enough at times. The Yanks are on the run in Virginia. Some say summer will see the finish of it."

"People said that last year," Francis added. "I've been in a fight or two, and they're always easier to begin than to end."

I wished we could have spoken longer that morning, but as activity ashore began, they went to work.

"No rest for a wharf rat," Francis insisted.

We saw the cousins again that afternoon. We liberated another half loaf from the galley, along with some roast beef. They accepted it less reluctantly, deeming us friends now.

"I hope it will last you," I said, gripping our Confederate friends' wrists.

That day slaves had packed every inch of *Banshee*'s holds with cargo. In addition to casks of tobacco, the deck was stacked with bales of cotton.

"Piled like a hay wagon" was how Robert described it. "Fortunately we'll pass it on to the big ships at Nassau. I wouldn't care to face an Atlantic gale this heavy!"

Even our little cabin was packed with cargo. We

would sleep on deck, atop the cotton!

Odd as it seemed to try to run the gauntlet of Union ships with so ungainly a ship, it was impossible to pass up the chance to add to our profits. Robert purchased twenty bales with his own money, paying ten cents a pound, or fifty dollars Confederate, for each bale. He even talked me into risking the balance of my pay on the venture and purchased a solitary bale in my name.

"If we get through, you'll see a fivefold return on your investment," he told me. "Once that bale of yours arrives in Liverpool, it will bring fifty pounds sterling. Not bad for ten pounds risked in Wilmington."

"And if we don't get back?" I asked.

"Then you won't have need of cotton profits or pay, either one," he said, gripping my shoulders with his hands. "I feel lucky, though, Henry. And Steele's the best."

"I hope so," I said, frowning. "It isn't easy to steer a hay wagon through dozens of gunboats and cruisers!"

6

EVERY SAILOR IN Wilmington had his own opinion as to whether the inbound or outbound voyage was more dangerous. Some argued that the trip back to Nassau was more perilous because the Yankees would watch the mouth of the Cape Fear River the way a fox guards a rabbit hole. Moreover, the departing ships had to weave their way through the channel defenses and thus would not be able to use their speed. Captain Steele argued the opposite was true.

"Coming in, we have to feel our way along the coast," he told me. "You can't afford to be off course even a mile. There's no room to maneuver. And the enemy fleet's a mystery, Henry. You've got no idea where they are or which ships have their steam up."

Captain Steele had devised a clever strategy for eluding the Union blockaders. We worked our way down the Cape Fear River as dusk approached, then halted when we approached Fort Fisher. The captain sent Robert and our local pilot ashore. The pilot stayed while Robert returned with a report on the Union fleet from Colonel William Lamb, the Virginia lawyer in command at Fort Fisher. Robert produced a rough map of the various

Yankee ships. He then identified each of them from the official United States naval list. Except for two small gunboats, the other vessels were thoroughly described.

"There, that's the one," Captain Steele said, pointing to the map.

"*Minnesota*," Robert noted. "Three thousand three hundred and seven tons. Steam frigate. Has forty guns, including nine-, ten-, and eleven-inch Dahlgren smoothbores."

"Well, she won't need big guns to put holes in us," Captain Steele noted. "We're going right for her."

There was an odd sort of genius to the captain's plan. The flagship of the whole fleet, *Minnesota* was big and heavy. Although powerful, she depended on her sails for maximum speed. As a result, the admiral aboard dropped anchors at dusk and used his flagship as a command post for the squadron. The other ships gave *Minnesota* room because of the range of her guns. As a result, there was a gap of sorts in the blockade on either side of the big frigate. Once through the first line, we would have miles of ocean at our disposal and a dozen possible courses to choose in order to reach Nassau and safety.

"There's danger at first," Robert observed, "but we also have the guns of Fort Fisher to cover our retreat."

I couldn't see our stopping unless a Yankee shell struck. If that happened, there wouldn't be much retreating to be done!

"I'll say one thing about our captain," Tom declared. "He's not faint of heart. If you catch a lion napping, you can pull his tail and live to tell of it."

"Unless he wakes and clamps his jaws on to you!" George said nervously.

"True enough," Tom agreed. "The problem with taking on that particular ship is that *Minnesota* has led a charmed life. The day our big ironclad, CSS *Virginia,* sank *Cumberland* and *Congress, Minnesota* ran aground. She was stranded there, sure to be sunk the next day. But when *Virginia* returned, the Yankees had their own ironclad, *Monitor,* protecting the grounded ship. There was no getting around *Monitor,* and *Minnesota* lived to torment us anew."

John Bailey, who had served five years in the Royal Navy, complained that no ship in the fleet would be more alert than the flagship.

"No one's going asleep on watch with an admiral apt to strut onto the deck at any moment," John told me. "Keep a sharp watch, Henry. I'd like to spend a few pounds in Nassau before I take up residence in a Yank prison."

Captain Steele said much the same thing as night fell and he sent me up the mast to the forward lookout.

"Son, your eyes are my eyes. If you miss spotting a gunboat, we'll never get away with all this weight on deck."

I eyed *my* bale in particular. Mother would chuckle when she read of how my investment had brought her such a rich return. Now all we had to do was get it safely through the twenty or so Yank warships waiting to collect that same profit when they captured us.

I took my station atop the crosstie and peered out into the murky air beyond. I could feel *Banshee*'s pulse as her engines hummed into action. Our bow threaded its way down the channel and out into the Atlantic. To the left and right of us lay the signal lanterns of Federal gunboats. Ahead, high in her masts, hung more lanterns marking *Minnesota*'s position.

We slipped gracefully and quietly between the enemy gunboats and surged ahead toward the waiting flagship. All appeared to be going as planned. As with all plans, though, it was the unexpected that almost cost us our lives. A Yankee gunboat assigned to carry dispatches appeared from nowhere. I shouted the alarm, and Captain Steele put our helm over sharply. The gunboat crew was alert and had its forward gun loaded and ready. A blast came from no more than a hundred yards away, and a Yank shell roared past our stern and exploded on the far side of us.

Chaos quickly took hold of the whole Union fleet. Ships fired rockets into the air. Cannon boomed from every direction at once. But although the ocean was full of towering splashes, and my ears ached from the concussion of two near misses, Captain Steele kept his poise. He steered right at the flagship, then swung away safely. We passed so closely that George later swore he could count the buttons on the bridge officer's coat. We heard a fair amount of shouting and swearing aboard *Minnesota*, but I couldn't tell exactly what was said. A boy at sea heard things his mother never intended, and I suspected the admiral might well have been trying to expand my vocabulary that night.

There was a fairly rich mixture of language aboard *Banshee* as well. With Robert aboard, I dared not speak at all for fear of borrowing a choice phrase or two from George. Besides, I was so busy shouting locations of one ship or another that I scarcely had time for swearing.

We would certainly have been sunk that night had we made a hard run for it, as the enemy expected us to do.

Captain Steele outfoxed them, though. Once clear of the flagship, he cut his speed and went slow as death. The swiftest of the Yank gunboats raced past.

In the distance ships fired their cannon and continued to shoot rockets, but the action gradually drifted to the north and west of us. Captain Steele kept us parallel to the coast for a time before turning back toward open ocean. I spied the faint outline of a cruiser in the distance, but she never showed any sign of spotting us. When midnight arrived, I turned my post over to another sailor, Keith Davis, and joined Robert below. He had spread out a blanket for me atop the cotton bales, and I gladly took to my makeshift bed.

"You did good work this night, Henry," he said, gently touching my shoulder. "Captain Steele says you've earned a bonus."

"Well, I will have my cotton profit, won't I?" I asked.

"We're not in Nassau yet, cousin," he reminded me. "Ships have been caught on the high seas before. The danger's far from over."

"Speaking of danger, aren't you worried about your sleepwalking out here?" I asked. "You'd surely fall overboard and drown!"

"You would wake me."

"I'm afraid I'll sleep like the dead tonight, Robert."

"It's actually morning, Henry," he pointed out. "Here, if you're worried, slip this rope around your leg. I'll do the same."

"That way I'll wake," I said, nodding as I yawned.

"More likely, you'll go overboard with me," he whispered. "But at least I'll have company."

I managed a chuckle as I slipped the rope around my

ankle. Soon I was fast asleep and far beyond caring.

I awoke to find myself alone in my makeshift cotton bed. I glanced around and found *Banshee* lumbering along in a middling sea, bobbing like a heavy cork. The engines sounded labored. We were also raising a little smoke, which was dangerous.

"Well, you're alive after all," George called to me from the bow. He was at work securing two large casks of Virginia tobacco that had come loose during our adventurous run through the Yank fleet.

"Hungry too," I said, feeling my stomach rumble a bit more than normal. "I missed breakfast, I suppose."

"Cook put something by for you," George told me. "You're the talk of the ship, Henry, for spotting that gunboat. I'll bet Robert would offer you a sip of brandy to celebrate."

"Only if he has no thought of ever returning to Liverpool," I replied. "My mother made him swear to keep me away from spirits."

"You're a man of wealth and property now, Henry. It's time you set aside your worries over what your mother thinks."

"You say that only because you've never met my mother," I said, grinning. "Two Yankee fleets wouldn't stop her from blistering my bottom. You keep your Dublin ways, George O'Neal, and leave me to my own."

George pretended anger, but he was never good at pretense. In a quarter hour he was up and showing me how to retie the hitches and knots that kept our deck cargo out of the Atlantic. Meanwhile I slipped into the galley.

"You won't find much," Bob declared. "We were a bit

more generous than wise in Wilmington."

"Not even a leftover crust?" I asked.

"We're especially short of flour, you know. I can't understand what happened to all the bread I was baking. Half a loaf here; another there. You'd think we had elves!"

"I'm afraid that was my doing," I confessed. "There were a pair of boys in Wilmington—"

"The ones that sat on the barrels," he said, nodding. "I know. It's a hard thing, seeing lads so young with such a hunger. I used to find a way to sneak a bit of beef and bread to the young ones back in my days sailing to Boston. In the time of the starving."

"My father was a sailor back then," I said, sitting on a stool. "Long time ago, it seems. Drowned off the Massachusetts coast."

"Then you likely knew a bit of the starving yourself," Bob said. "Should've known. No boy who's ever been hungry will see another go shy of what he can spare. Here, Henry." The cook reached into a drawer and produced as if by magic a slice of bread, some roast beef, and three raw carrots. "For your eyes," he explained.

I ate hungrily while Bob recounted his days aboard the emigrant ships crossing back and forth from Liverpool to America. I had aunts and an uncle who had made that crossing, but no one had ever told me of its hazards and hardships. When Bob finished, I studied his face.

"You've been hungry too," I said.

"What boy born in Wales hasn't been?" he asked. "But it's the perils of youth that make for strong men, Henry. There are few trades better for man or boy than the sea. You'll never run out of new places to visit, and you'll make all manner of friends. There's a future to it too. Just look there at Captain Steele. He wasn't born to money. He learned his trade as you and I, and see him now! As good a captain as runs the blockade."

We were three days crossing open ocean to Nassau. In all that time no one ever took a full breath. I stood lookout for four hours at a time, and a more tedious task was never conceived. I scanned the horizon from left to right and back again every few minutes. Someone would climb the mast with food at mid-watch, and I had a water flask that I usually emptied before coming down. Tired as I sometimes got, I could not relax my guard. Each speck on the horizon meant danger. Extra lookouts took position when any sign of another ship appeared. No hint of trouble escaped Captain Steele's attention. Most of the time it was only another steamer off to break the blockade. Twice we saw cruisers, but they chased us only a short while before turning away. Even laden as we were, there was no catching us from so far away.

We entered Nassau in triumph. No one had ever seen a ship piled so high with cargo elude the Yank cruisers, and we created a stir. Myself, I only wanted to enjoy a good night's sleep. Even as the work gangs began removing our cargo, Robert made arrangements for the rental of several rooms in town.

"A man of wealth can afford a real bed," he said, showing me the invoice for my bale of cotton, valued at fifty pounds sterling, consigned to a Liverpool-bound merchantman.

Actually Robert paid for almost everything, insisting

that I send my wages home. He did allow me to keep five pounds, together with ten shillings Captain Steele handed me as a reward for spotting the gunboat. I spent the money on a pair of new shoes, some cotton shirts more appropriate to the sultry summer climate, and a suit of clothes fit for the celebration Robert was hosting at a nearby hotel the following night.

The party was supposed to be a small gathering of some of the other captains and mates, together with the port officials. But as had happened in Wilmington, we had a number of uninvited guests. First the officers of a United States steam sloop appeared. Then the American consul, Charles Fornier, and his family arrived. I had not been there five minutes before his niece Andrea clamped on to my arm and dragged me aside.

"Well, I see you are celebrating your piracy," she said.

"What?" I gasped.

"How can your cousin flaunt his successes in the face of my country's misery? You English say you are friends of America, and yet you aid the rebellion that threatens our nation's very existence!"

"I'm sorry you feel I'm threatening you," I said, prying her fingers from my arm. "I'm not the one launching an attack, though."

"No? Isn't this party a celebration of your success, an invitation for others to join your enterprise? Tell me, Henry, do you know what will happen when we catch you? Do you think you will be allowed to return to England? No, you will be put in prison, where you will probably grow sick or even die. No one talks of such things when they enlist young sailors. No, it's all glory and riches until you're caught."

"I can't imagine why that should concern you," I told her. "If I'm an enemy of your country, you should be glad if that happened."

"I wouldn't be glad," she said, sighing. "Captain Mills is recruiting sailors. You might sign on with him."

"Andrea, I give up," I said, raising my arms in mock surrender. "Isn't one war enough? I don't know a handful of people in Nassau, and I don't want to be arguing with the prettiest one. I just want to enjoy myself a short while. Would you like to join me?"

She looked down at me with her brooding eyes. I wasn't sure whether she was going to agree or find a harpoon to ram through my forehead.

"New shoes?" she asked.

"New everything," I said, turning so she could see how the coat fit. "Except the same old Henry Severn's inside."

"There's music playing. Do you know how to dance?"

"Not to that sort of music," I said, laughing.

"Willing to try?" she asked.

"I've done more foolish things," I told her.

But as it turned out, I hadn't. I never did learn to match her steps, and her toes suffered as a result. Still, we kept an unofficial truce that night, and I think Andrea even enjoyed herself a little. For myself, I found it a moment of peace squeezed into a month of hard work and unrelenting danger. Still, it was only a moment. Soon we would be back at sea.

7

IT WAS A STRANGE life I led in Nassau. One day I was dressed in a fashionable coat, wearing new shoes and stepping on the toes of a consul's niece. The next found me hip deep in a coal bunker, choking on black dust.

Coaling was one of the more tiresome tasks a steamer undertook. Before we departed Nassau, it was critical to fill our bunkers with good Welsh coal. We would have a hard time replenishing our stocks in Wilmington, and the quality would never meet Mr. Erskine's standards. Good coal burned hot and clean, leaving only a trace of smoke for enemy lookouts to spot. With *Banshee*'s temperamental engines, we needed the best coal we could find to obtain her maximum speed.

It was hard duty, shoveling coal into *Banshee*'s hungry furnaces, and a third of our crew were stokers, the poor wretches who spent their whole watch feeding the engines. To expect them to refill the bunkers while the rest of us lay about was unreasonable, and Captain Steele ordered everyone except the officers and Bob Jones to lend a hand.

In all my fourteen years I never knew such hard work. Even with George shoveling alongside, I couldn't find a way to make the time pass quickly. Soon my arms ached, and every inch of me was coated with coal dust.

"Now you know why the stokers strip before doing it," George said, laughing as he marked a circle on my forehead.

"You're no better," I said, painting him a mustache. "If you close your eyes, I won't be able to see you!"

The worst part of coaling was trying to get clean afterward. The stokers plunged overboard and scrubbed themselves in the harbor. I was a little too modest to join them. Instead I tried to scrub the filth from my hide in a wooden tub in Robert's rooms. Even using the best soap in Nassau, I couldn't get every trace of it off. George, with his red hair and light complexion, fared even worse. He had one streak of black down his back that resisted all our efforts. Once we left port, he tied a rope around his waist and jumped into the sea. The salt water finally cleansed him. It looked like fun, and I took a turn afterward.

That afternoon we sighted two sharks. George and I exchanged nervous glances.

"A shark will make you forget all about a bit of coal dust," Bob remarked when he brought food up from the galley that afternoon. "They bite clean, though. I knew a fellow had a leg took off just above the knee. Shark ate well that day."

It ate better than I did. I confess that Bob's tale left me with little of my usual appetite.

Despite rough seas, our second run to Wilmington went rather smoothly. We all knew our ship better, and even the engines appeared to be settling down. Captain Steele let me have a turn at the wheel, steering *Banshee* half of the midday watch. George continued to teach me knots and hitches while Tom showed me how to read charts.

It seemed odd, but I saw less and less of Robert. He was usually with the captain, making plans or discussing *Banshee*'s shortcomings. Williams Brothers was joining two other firms to build several new ships, and Robert was determined to remedy all earlier mistakes.

I passed most of my time with George, learning a sailor's craft and alternately swapping my stories of Liverpool for his Dublin tales. Robert had sent my first letters to Liverpool, and I took a little time each evening to write a few lines. I had been gone two months. Even though I was growing accustomed to life at sea, I missed my family.

Sometimes, when no one was watching, I would sit alone with Colleen's jumper and try to sniff out the odors of home from the Scottish wool. I closed my eyes and tried to imagine how Tim was faring at the office, sitting in those high chairs as his mind worked through the long columns of numbers. And Francis! I hoped he was doing better than that pitiful boy I'd met in Wilmington. Mostly, though, I saw Mother sitting beside the fire, chatting with Colleen while gazing at the photograph resting on the mantel.

"It was a good notion, Colleen," I whispered to the wind.

Two days out of Nassau we encountered a gale. I'd never seen wind blow so hard, and it was impossible to stay dry anywhere. Mr. Erskine had the pumps working every hour, and that kept most of the leaking under control. But it did nothing to protect us when we went out onto the deck.

"Rig ropes," Captain Steele ordered. George and I, being off duty at the time, took on the task of placing a network of ropes along either side of the deck. The lines proved helpful to the men as they made their way fore or aft to change lookouts or to attend to their bodily functions. Up on the crosstie, where I stood watch, there was no protection from the wind and waves. My eyes stung from the wicked spray, and my shirt was ripped to shreds. There was a chill in the air too, and I returned to the deck half-frozen after every watch.

"I'll send some tea up with you next time," Bob offered as I thawed out beside the warmth of his cooking fire.

"No point," I told him. "I need my hands free to hang on to the mast. The wind nearly blew me loose once!"

The storm was a mixed blessing for a lookout. While it concealed *Banshee* from our enemies, it hid other ships from us. Captain Steele reminded us that a collision at sea usually meant drowned sailors. I couldn't help but recall Fa's death, and I took my station with growing dread.

Our luck seemed to hold, though. *Banshee* continued onward despite the heavy sea. Then it happened. I was on watch, but all I heard was a clatter of pewter plates. It was morning, when there was no tea to greet the first watch, before we realized Bob was missing. George found three plates on deck, and I noticed a bit of torn cloth.

"Poor fellow," Captain Steele said, frowning. "He's gone overboard."

I felt as if a brick had struck my head. Bob? Gone?

"Can't we look for him?" I asked. "Maybe he's out there, swimming."

The sea had grown calm, and I scanned the horizon for some trace of the grinning Welshman.

"You remember what it was like last night, Henry," Robert said, shaking his head.

I nodded. Thinking back to when we received news of Fa's drowning, I crossed myself and whispered a prayer. George did likewise.

"I wish I'd talked to him more," I said, thinking of all the times he had hidden a bit of bread for us or heated some stew during a midnight watch. "It must have been a horrible way to die, drowning all alone, not even noticed."

"Oh, I don't know that one way's worse than another," George told me. "I never knew a man more at peace with himself than Bob. I'm no cook myself, and I don't care for kitchen work. Bob never minded a bit of it, though."

It wasn't long before we realized just how much we missed Bob. Charlie Herring, one of the engine crew, took over in the galley, but he was a disappointment.

"A herring's a fish, isn't it?" John Bailey asked after tasting a bite of Charlie's stew. "Here's one should've been thrown back."

Afterward a third of the crew was retching, and the rest were running to and from the heads!

"You can cook a little, can't you?" Robert asked me after we had finally purged ourselves of the last of the stew.

"I can fry bacon and eggs," I answered, "bake biscuits and boil potatoes."

"You're cook then," Robert announced. "So long as you don't poison us all, you'll be an improvement."

I accepted my fate with some reluctance. Even with

George assigned to help, I was far from content. Back in Cork, when I was only a little boy, I'd done some of the cooking on days when Mother and Colleen were past weary. After burning a few biscuits, I learned to keep the fire down, and there wasn't much to frying eggs. I judged us a day out of Wilmington at the most. We could survive that long on what I could cook.

The crew treated me like salvation in the flesh. I couldn't believe anyone would celebrate a few eggs and slices of bacon, but they did. I boiled some vegetables for our supper, but I dared not try anything fancy. As it was, I passed most of two straight watches cooking, with George busy most of that time scraping plates and scouring pots.

"I don't see how Bob managed," he told me. "I'm worn down to a nub."

For me, it was only worse. At dusk we approached the blockade. Tired though I was, Captain Steele ordered me to my lookout post, and I struggled up the mast. We were completely enclosed in darkness. The late spring air was hot and heavy. It did little to chase away my fatigue.

That night the Yankee ships were showing lights, and it seemed that Tom Burroughs saw each and every one of them. Captain Steele took the helm himself, and we slipped past one shadowy vessel after another. Then, when it seemed as if we would work our way free of the enemy and cruise safely up the Cape Fear channel, *Banshee* shuddered. There was a terrible ripping and splintering of wood from our left side. I glanced down in time to see one of the steel floats on the portside paddle wheel rip into the paddle box, tearing it apart.

By the time Captain Steele recognized the trouble,

Mr. Erskine had already shut down the engines. He was on deck a moment later, gazing at the wrecked paddle box in dismay. In a matter of minutes half the crew was on deck.

"No time's to be lost," Mr. Erskine said, gathering the engineers. "Ready some ropes. I must get that float off before we founder."

It was a moment of great trial for all of us. The engineers rigged a cover that they draped over the paddle box. Two of them then went over the side. While one man removed pieces of splintered wood, the other tried to detach the damaged float. Extra lookouts were posted, and all hands were ordered to keep quiet. Sound carried far on such a quiet night, though, and it wasn't possible to stay completely silent. Mr. Erskine needed to instruct his engineers on how to repair the damage.

It was inevitable that the Yankees would hear something. The miracle was that they gave us a third of an hour to work unmolested. I spied the first shadowy form no more than a hundred yards away.

Lord protect us, I thought. I then called below, and all eyes turned to where a Yankee cruiser broke through the darkness. The enemy ship was so close that I could see the big pivot gun on her stern! I didn't spot a single lookout, though. The cruiser steamed past us, and I breathed a sigh of relief.

At any moment another ship might appear, or perhaps a cannon shot would put an end to our troubles. I wouldn't have been surprised had either occurred. The only sound I heard, however, was a solitary splash as the broken float struck the ocean and began its descent to the bottom. Mr. Erskine ordered his men back on deck, and before long we were steaming once again.

Our ordeal was far from over, though. A half hour without steam had drawn us dangerously close to the coast. Once we resumed our journey, three enemy gunboats took notice. The eastern horizon was showing the first traces of dawn, and we no longer had the advantage of darkness. Yank gunners opened fire when we were still seven miles from the safety of Fort Fisher's protective guns.

What followed was a true sea chase. With a damaged left paddle wheel, *Banshee* steamed unevenly. It took every ounce of Captain Steele's skill to keep us on anything resembling a straight course. All the while gunboats opened fire from seemingly every direction. Shell splashes peppered us with spray, and wicked metal splinters battered our deck. Up in my lookout perch, I felt utterly helpless. I kept expecting someone to shout for me to come down. After all, the gun flashes marked each and every gunboat's location.

Tom Burroughs then did something odd. He raced forward and lit two signal lamps. While other blockade-runners frequently signaled the rebels ashore to mark the channel, Tom had always argued against showing lights. "You're only inviting gunfire," he had told me.

But this time the signals had a most welcome effect. No sooner did Tom swing the first lantern than we heard a resounding boom from our right. One of Fort Fisher's big cannon belched smoke and flame. Moments later a shell exploded fifteen feet from the nearest gunboat. The Yank vessel veered away, and we raced past.

Two other gunboats attempted to block our passage ahead, but those Fort Fisher gunners knew their business.

The thin-sided gunboats were no match for the fort's massive batteries, and near misses convinced them of the merits of withdrawal.

When we passed safely into the channel of the Cape Fear River, I finally caught my breath. I was soaked with perspiration, and my heart was pounding. Robert called to me from the deck, but I was unable to muster the strength to climb down. George came up and helped me to the deck.

"You all right?" Robert asked as I stumbled toward our cabin.

"Just tired," I told him. "It was a long night."

"And a long day before that," Robert observed. "Get some rest, Henry. You've earned it."

"Who's going to get breakfast ready?" I asked.

"Someone else," George said as he dragged me along to my hammock.

8

I AWOKE TO FIND it was late afternoon. We were already tied up to a wharf in Wilmington. When I rolled out of my hammock, I discovered George asleep on the deck outside my cabin. "George?" I asked.

"You're up," he said, rubbing the sleep from his eyes. "I was wondering if you would sleep until Sunday."

"I'm the one who's getting *you* up," I pointed out.

"You haven't spent all morning unloading cargo," he replied.

"I would have if anybody had roused me," I argued. "I slept through everything?" I asked, pointing to the circle of slaves enjoying a break from their labors.

"Captain Steele ordered me to stand guard at your door and keep anybody from disturbing you. It wasn't easy. We had to make do with cold biscuits and watery tea."

"I'll see if I can—"

"Captain Steele's gone ashore to hire a cook," George explained. "He says he can't spare you from the lookout post. To tell the truth, though, I don't think he likes eggs."

"I'm not much of a cook," I confessed.

"No, you're not," George agreed.

Our stay in Wilmington was a short one. The skies

had grown cloudy, and all the signs of a fierce storm were in the air. Captain Steele was in a hurry to take advantage of the dark skies and wary Yankee captains. Playing our earlier trick, we slipped past the enemy flagship without so much as a wave this time. Three days later we were back in Nassau.

I breathed a long sigh of relief when we unloaded *Banshee*'s deck cargo. I had staked every penny of my wages on deck cargo, and the profits would be considerable when the cotton was sold in Liverpool. Robert offered to advance me all or part of it to spend in Nassau, but I didn't need new clothes or rich food. I worried about my family, and I instructed Robert to turn over the money to Mother as before.

I was especially glad of the decision when I discovered seven letters were waiting for me. There were three from Mother, two from Colleen, and two from Tim. Mother wrote of how well everyone was doing. Tim was enrolled at a good school starting in September, and Francis was growing taller daily. She also said there were stories of captured blockade-runners in the newspaper. Crewmen taken prisoner, she said, faced mistreatment from the Yanks.

We have money enough now, she wrote. *It's time you came home.*

Colleen echoed Mother's feelings. Her words tore at my heart.

You should see how Mother stares at your picture. Sometimes I see her crying as she reads your letters. You don't write half so often as she'd like!

Tim mainly spoke of the excitement that swept through Williams Brothers each time a cargo of cotton arrived in port. While Robert and I were making a few hundred pounds, the company was earning tens of thousands!

It's just money, though, he wrote near the end of his second letter. *We all miss you. Mother cries a lot, and Francis says we haven't had any luck fishing since you left. Maybe you should come home.*

Robert mentioned it too. "The best days of running the blockade are behind us," he said. "Each time out we come across more Yank ships. And now they're bigger and faster."

There was another peril awaiting us too. Summer arrived, bringing with it the wrath of Yellow Jack, as yellow fever was called in the Bahamas. The sickness stalked sailors like a dark cloud, and no ship docking at Nassau avoided it forever. Confederate authorities ordered blockade-runners to drop anchor in the Cape Fear River in a quarantine line that delayed unloading cargoes. Nobody made more than a single run under the monthly moonless period anymore.

Nevertheless, our third trip to Wilmington was our easiest. We spotted only one other ship on the open ocean, and it proved to be British. Tom found us a hole in the blockade that seemed no bigger than the eye of a needle, but we threaded our way safely in and out.

Summer found the Confederacy changed. Wilmington had once echoed with the boasts of rebel officers and politicians. High hopes had filled the population after General Robert E. Lee invaded Pennsylvania, but a disastrous defeat at Gettysburg had shattered dreams of imminent southern independence. The people seemed to be preparing for an even longer war.

Even an Irish-born boy of fourteen could spot the sour gaze of Wilmington's women. North Carolina had lost more than its share of young men in Pennsylvania, and hardly anyone I met didn't have a brother, father, or cousin among the dead or wounded. Boys no older than fifteen or sixteen manned the batteries along the Cape Fear River, and even some of the officers were beardless boys not so much older than George and I.

After a particularly harrowing tale told to us by a one-legged veteran, I exchanged an uneasy look with George. "Have you ever imagined what it's like to die?" I asked.

"Oh, I should be dead a dozen times already," George answered. "I never saw the point of wondering what it's like. You find out sooner than you wish."

I tried to keep my growing sense of gloom out of my letters home. I couldn't help writing about George, though, or our close calls running the blockade. Mother scolded me for putting myself in peril, especially for money.

We have enough now. Come home, she pleaded. But I was as much a part of *Banshee* as her keel. I owed it to Robert to stay aboard. I hated the notion of leaving Captain Steele and Tom without their best lookout. Most of all, I had a true friend in George O'Neal. As long as he stayed, I wouldn't leave.

We started our fourth run to Wilmington that August, leaving a Nassau thoroughly beset by fever and carrying desperately needed rifles, percussion caps, and gunpowder in every free space on the ship. Captain Steele ordered the deck kept clear, but we even had two boxes of Enfield rifles in the galley.

I thought how Bob would have complained about

that. Our new cook, a white-haired old rebel named Jubal Wallace, never uttered a single complaint against those rifles. "I have five grandsons under the Confederate colors," he told me. "They need those guns."

The trouble began when we approached the mouth of the Cape Fear River. The outer line of blockaders seemed oddly absent, and the solitary steamship we spied failed to notice our passage. When we saw the faint outline of land through the midnight darkness, there were no signal lamps or watch fires. From my lookout post I heard Tom utter a particularly loud curse.

I soon learned why. Three trips in and out of the blockade had taught me the lay of the land, and we were nowhere near where we should have been. A signal rocket exploded in the air more than ten miles to the south, and its faint glow told me we were considerably north of our usual mark. I wasn't concerned because we could still work our way alongshore until we fell under the protective covering fire of Fort Fisher's big guns.

Any thought of safety quickly vanished. The dark outline of a Yankee cruiser appeared on our port bow, and I shouted an alarm. The cruiser fired off a rocket moments later, and I could see men scurrying about on deck. We had only a few heartbeats before cannon would open fire.

Captain Steele faced an impossible choice. Although we were at full steam, we couldn't elude the cruiser. We could go inside her, close to shore, or turn outside and risk encountering the rest of the Yank blockading squadron. I had overheard him talking to Robert about that very maneuver a dozen times or more, so I wasn't surprised to see *Banshee* break toward the Carolina coast. We risked grounding, and with our hull painted gray, we would be outlined against the watch fires and signal lamps up ahead. Still, if we were holed, there was a chance of beaching the ship and escaping into friendly arms. Among the blockading Yanks, capture was the best we could hope for if we were sunk.

Banshee's quick actions caught the Yankees off guard, and we managed to pull even with the cruiser and slip past before she could react. We were close enough to hear shouts and taunts by the Yank sailors.

"Stop that steamer or I will sink you!" shouted an officer from the cruiser's deck.

"Sink us if you will!" old Jubal replied. "No prize money for you then."

It was a treat to see Captain Steele and Mr. Erskine work their magic. *Banshee* slowed as she slipped past the Yank guns, and they fired their first broadside into the ocean ahead of us. We then returned to full steam, surging along as the Yank gunners hurried to reload. Then, as they were ready to fire, Captain Steele swung us about like a corkscrew, heading out to sea a moment before turning back toward the coast.

The Yankees missed us badly again, but the third time they fired their guns slowly, in turn. I counted six of them. The last two nearly caught us. Shell splashes drenched everyone on deck, and metal splinters bounced off our hull. Amid blasting cannon and signal rockets, I read the enemy ship's nameplate. *Niphon!*

Niphon was a new screw steamer, driven by a propeller instead of paddle wheels. She was actually only about three-fourths our length. Small as she was, she equaled our speed and clung to our heels as we fought to leave her behind.

"Come down from there, Henry!" Captain Steele shouted as a Yank shell whined past our stern. "He's getting the range."

I realized how dangerous it was for me, sitting alone in the lookout post, and I tried to muster the courage to start down. With *Banshee* gyrating in three directions at once, though, I couldn't get a toehold on the foremast. My legs dangled below me, and I hugged the mast with both arms.

"Hang on," George shouted. He was climbing the mast before I had a chance to wave him off. As the Yanks fired again, he tore me loose and dragged me along toward the deck. It was a miracle we weren't killed, for the Yanks shot away the foremast and exploded a shell in our coal bunkers seconds after we touched the deck.

Banshee shook from stem to stern, and the whole crew hugged the deck. *Niphon* fired canister at us, blasting away the deck fittings and splintering the top of the steerage cabin. I could see boarders filing into two longboats, and I imagined our end was near. *Banshee* turned sideways, and I worried Captain Steele or the helmsman was dead.

"The wheel!" Captain Steele shouted.

I saw the helmsman, Keith Davis, flat on the deck. Robert raced for the cabin, and I ran after him. As new Yank shells straddled our pitiful little ship, we arrived in the battered cabin. Robert stopped the wheel, and I stared out the window at the coast falling away on our starboard side.

"Turn it to the right!" I yelled, and Robert soon had us back on course. *Niphon*'s crew, who imagined us at their mercy, had already started toward us in their boats.

The steamer had to slow down to recover its men, and we finally pulled away.

The drama wasn't over, though. First another cruiser fired a shell into our bow. Then a side-wheeler tried to ram us. I'm not sure how we eluded that one because she was close enough to spit at! We still might have been sunk if not for Fort Fisher's alert gunners. They opened up at maximum range. For a few moments our pursuers stayed with us. Then one of Colonel Lamb's big guns smashed into the closest gunboat. The others turned away.

We didn't exactly steam into Wilmington this time. We more or less limped. Worse, the rebel surgeons ordered us to join the quarantine line, and we had no help making repairs. Mr. Erskine fumed, saying the ungrateful rebels might cost us our ship and cargo. But when we learned that twenty-nine people had died in Wilmington the week before from yellow fever, we swallowed our bitterness.

The days spent at anchor in the sweltering summer heat left us all tired and irritable. Mr. Erskine drafted George and me to help shovel coal from the damaged bunkers, and that only made us filthy as well as miserable. Our only break was at twilight, when we would jump from the stern and swim off the coal dust.

After ten days on the quarantine line we were finally allowed to tie up at a Wilmington wharf. With a full moon in the sky and days of repairs awaiting us, I decided it was time to have a good look at Wilmington. With Robert's permission, George and I headed off into town.

We had told Robert and Captain Steele that we wanted only to stretch our legs and get our hair cut, but the truth was that we wanted a real look at the Confederate port. There were still traces of the prewar Wilmington, a city of fine houses and aristocrats. But mostly we passed gaming houses and saloons. Homemade corn liquor was available, as were fine wines and scotch whiskey brought in by the blockade-runners. George favored sampling a bottle, but I knew better. Robert wrote Mother nearly as often as I did, and one word of drinking would land me back in Liverpool forever.

We did treat ourselves to a meal of grilled trout, boiled potatoes, and a strange kind of bean called a black-eyed pea. A pretty red-haired girl of seventeen named Kate Ennis served us. When she learned we were Irish, she brought us a pitcher of cool tea and entertained us with tales of her own journey from Galway to New York and then down the coast to North Carolina.

"To hear some people, every Irish man, woman, and child to leave the island has gone to New York or Boston," she grumbled. "Why, there are plenty of us down South as well. Have you heard of Patrick Cleburne, the best general we've got in the West? And now you brave lads come to help us."

I was a little uneasy, hearing myself praised in such a fashion. It was money that drew me aboard *Banshee*. After our recent troubles I had seen enough Yank cannon to last a lifetime.

"It's a hard life breaking through the blockade," George told Kate. "Did you know they practically shot Henry here right from our foremast!"

"It's true," I said. "George saved me, though."

"You wouldn't be from Cork now, would you?" she asked.

"I would," I confessed. "And I know all about the Blarney stone. I've never even seen it!"

"Some have no need," she said, laughing.

We reluctantly left Kate to her other customers after her boss scolded her. George and I then made our way to a barber's shop, where we had baths and got our hair cut. We also paused to have our pictures taken by a local photographer. I intended to send mine home. George left his with Kate.

"She's too old for you," I said, shaking my head.

He just grinned. "There's scarcely a grown man left under sixty years of age, Henry," George pointed out. "You heard that barber. I'll be needing a shave soon."

"Not *that* soon," I said, laughing.

It was just as well that we had a bit of a holiday in town. The next day, as I sat beside Robert, tallying figures, I heard shouts of alarm from the docks. A pillar of smoke rose from our wharf, and I instantly darted out to determine the cause. To my shock and horror, *Banshee* was a solid sheet of flame. Something had ignited the deck cargo.

Robert joined me, but he had no idea of what to do. *Banshee* was loaded with cotton and turpentine, and both were feeding the flames. We looked on helplessly as our ship became an inferno. Captain Steele had been visiting with the mayor down the road, and he came marching out, barking orders to anyone who would listen.

"You there!" he shouted. "Henry! Come along now!"

I followed obediently.

The rest of the crew were running toward the ship, but no one could get aboard because of the fire. Fortunately Captain Halpin of *Eugenie,* the ship tied aft of us, had acted quickly. He had several men row him alongside *Banshee,* and he cut the cable so that the ship's stern swung into the wind. The breeze drew the worst of the fire away from the ship's vitals.

Captain Steele, aided by a fire brigade and their steam hoses, forced his way aboard ship. Townspeople and sailors formed bucket brigades to help. I finally jumped onto the blackened deck, armed with a wet blanket, and began extinguishing bits of burning cotton.

While the older men pushed blazing bales into the river, George and I tried to salvage what we could. Although the fire had burned fiercely and hot, our actual damage wasn't too great. As the last flickers died away, we found ourselves relieved that it wasn't worse. The new foremast was charred but undamaged. The turtleback hump forward was gone, but the decks and bulwarks survived.

"Pity we had the deck cargo aboard," Robert said, shaking his head. Two of those bales were mine, so I too regretted the loss.

Confederate authorities suspected one of the slaves who loaded the cargo might have set the fire, but no culprit came forward. Whatever proof may have existed went up in smoke.

Robert spoke for all of us when he thanked our Wilmington friends for their help and ordered old Jubal to prepare a luncheon for everyone.

"It was only cotton," he told me that night. "No lives were lost, and we still have our ship."

I nodded my agreement. Still, I wished I had my two bales, for I had no money to buy replacements. I had profits enough, though, and I deemed it a cautionary event. On all our remaining trips the Confederate government insisted on shipping its own deck cotton, leaving little room for Robert to place his own bales aboard. For me, there was no room at all.

We were an entire day repainting and a day after that taking on another load of deck cargo. By the time the moon began to wane, we were once again steaming down the Cape Fear River. Three days later we were safely in Nassau again.

9

THAT AUGUST OF 1863 found Nassau choked with heat and suffering anew from yellow fever. Some ships had shifted their base to Bermuda in hope of eluding the silent killer, but Yellow Jack beat them there. Whole crews came down with it. Ours was no exception.

No one knew exactly what caused the disease, but it had plagued the Americas for as long as anyone in Nassau could remember. Sailors called it Yellow Jack because of the small yellow flags that ships flew on the quarantine line. It was seemingly everywhere that summer. I was the first of *Banshee*'s crew to catch it.

It seemed odd to me at the time. We had been in Nassau two whole days without any problems. Most of the ships carrying fever brought it with them into port. George and I had finished our duties unloading cargo and were exploring the town. I felt a little dizzy, and I sat beside the street, rubbing my temples as if that would ease the pain welling up inside my head.

"Henry?" George asked, leaning over.

"I think I'm sick," I told him.

I'm not entirely sure what happened next. My head was pounding. My stomach ached. Somehow George got me to Robert's rooms. When I regained my senses, a smiling young black woman was wiping sweat from my forehead with a damp cloth.

"You have the fever," she whispered.

"I'm going to die?" I asked her.

"Oh, not everybody dies," she said, shaking her head in an exaggerated manner. "Not at all. You're young. Me, I have it when I was twelve. All my brothers and sisters too. None of us die. Now we are safe. You can get the yellow jack only once. Then you are safe."

"Like measles?" I asked.

"Like measles," she agreed, nodding. "You been sick two days now. Soon you will be better."

"Or dead?" I asked.

"Oh, I don't think you will die. No, not you. Your cousin says you are too wicked to die young."

"He what?"

"You rest now. Leave Patricia to make you well. In a little while I will bring you some broth. Yes? You're hungry?"

Her words had an odd effect on me. I hadn't felt hungry before, but suddenly it was as though I had a hole in my belly.

"Yes, Patricia. I'd like that."

"Good," she said, patting my chest. "It's a good sign."

Perhaps it was, for after sipping the broth, I started to regain my senses. I could hear coughing in the other room and learned that Robert was also sick.

"Not so bad as you were," Patricia told me later. "Not everyone has even fever. It's a good thing to catch it when you are young and strong. Then you don't have more trouble from it later."

I had a hard time feeling very grateful for catching it, though. My back felt as if someone had bounced a cannonball off it, and I was wet all over with sweat. The broth settled uneasily in my belly, and I fought the urge to vomit.

Patricia was like an angel come to earth. I later discovered the governor, deeming Robert an important person, had sent her to us. It wasn't the first time I had benefited from Robert's help in a crisis, but it was never more welcome. Patricia fed me, bathed me, and even shared some of her grandfather's stories of his pirate days. It wasn't altogether comfortable, being treated like an infant when you were fourteen years old, but I was in no position to argue.

She was right on the mark where Robert and I were concerned. The fourth day after collapsing in the street I managed to rise from my bed and enjoy a warm bath—without female assistance! Robert was up a day later. Although Patricia worried over us another few days, it proved unnecessary. We had survived the scourge of tropical America.

By then yellow fever had worked its way through most of the crew. Aside from old Jubal and three stokers, who had fought off the fever years before, the whole crew was sick. Counting Robert and me, twenty-eight of us caught the disease. By the time I was well enough to walk to the ship, five men had died.

George was the last to take sick. With Robert's permission, I brought him into town and gave him my bed. Although he was two inches shorter and a few months younger than I was, he had always seemed the strong, indestructible one. Yellow fever hit him hard.

"I don't like this," Patricia told me when she examined George. "He is turning yellow."

"Is that bad?" I asked.

"Why do you think they call it the *yellow* fever?" she asked. "He is very sick."

By that time Patricia was spending most of her hours at the ship, tending others. Being safe from the fever myself, I took on the task of nursing George. It wasn't hard work. I just gave him some cool tea or spring water when he asked for it and kept a damp rag on his forehead. Sometimes I talked to him, but most of the time he was mumbling to his mother or thrashing his arms about.

The fourth day he became calm. The fever broke, and his eyes cleared. "I've got it," he said, staring into my eyes. "Henry, is that you?"

"Nobody else would claim to be me," I answered. "You're better. Feel like sipping some broth?"

He turned paler than usual and shook his head. "I can't," he said, trying to sit up. "Maybe later."

I tried to be hopeful as I sat with him that day, jabbering about home and recounting our adventures.

"You shouldn't be here," he finally told me. "You'll catch it."

"You get it only once," I told him. "I can't catch it off you."

"Once can be enough," he said, sighing. "I'm glad you're here, though, Henry. I'd miss hearing an Irish tongue, even one from Cork."

"Oh, there's more Liverpool in me now than Cork," I told him. "Mixed in with a portion of Wilmington and Nassau."

"You'll make a true sailor. Nowhere entirely at home, but at ease everywhere."

"I thought so once," I said, gazing out the window toward the harbor. "Now I'm far from certain of it. Home has its comforts."

"But the sea has adventure," he said, grinning.

"Like almost getting shot from the foremast?" I asked.

"I got you down in time," he reminded me. "Well, I suppose you're returning the favor, helping me slip away from the yellow jack."

"Doing my best," I assured him.

Later that afternoon Robert dragged a tub in, and together we got George out of his clothes and into the cooling water. Before, with a sheet covering him, I hadn't noticed how yellow and shrunken he had become. There had never been a lot to George, but I doubt he weighed ninety pounds that day. He lacked the strength to wash himself, and I was ill at ease doing it.

"It doesn't matter," George finally said, clasping my hand weakly. "I'll be stronger tomorrow."

He wasn't, though. The fever returned. It was as if the yellow fever were eating away at his insides. I could barely feel his pulse, and he began vomiting darkish goo.

"Do me a favor?" he finally whispered.

"Anything," I promised.

"Go see if you can locate a priest. I'm not religious, mind you. It's only that my mother—"

"I know, George," I said, sighing. "I haven't been to mass in a while, but I know where to go."

So that afternoon I made my way through the busy streets of Nassau to the old Spanish church. As luck would have it, I found myself greeted by a young Irish priest named Father Matthew. As I explained the purpose of my visit, he nodded solemnly. "You come from the south coast?" he asked. "Waterford?"

"Cork," I explained. "My friend George is from Dublin, but we can't all be perfect."

"I'm a Dubliner myself," Father Matthew explained. "Just let me get my things."

We hurried through town, and arrived at George's bedside to find him quiet but alert. The priest sent me outside. The two of them spoke for a time. Then Father Matthew took me back in.

"He's at peace, Henry," he told me. "He's confessed, and I've given him the last rites. I wish I could stay a bit longer, but—"

"I'll be here," I assured him. "Thank you for coming."

I offered him the five shillings I had in my pockets, but he wouldn't take the money. "You may have need of it," he told me.

It was as difficult a time as I'd known in my whole life, sitting with George and waiting for the end. Robert came in and sat with us for an hour, but he finally left.

"I'm sorry, George," I told him when we were alone again. "You brought me down from the mast, but I wasn't able to save you."

"You've been a good friend, though," he said, shuddering. "A brother."

He asked one final favor of me, to write his parents and send them his wages. As I sat there, fighting to find the words, he seemed to brighten.

"Just tell my mother that I've confessed my sins," he said. "Tell her the priest was here."

"It won't be the same without you, George," I said

after writing the letter. "Who will teach me the rest of my knots?"

"You know most of what's important, Henry. Sing me a song of home?"

I never was much of a singer, and with my voice halfway through changing, I produced an odd array of whines. Nevertheless, I sang one of Mother's favorites.

George managed a smile and closed his eyes. His chest rose and fell three or four times. Then it remained still. I searched his wrist for a pulse but found none.

"George?" I whispered.

He was gone.

Father Matthew arranged a funeral mass, and Robert had a stone marker erected in the churchyard with George's name and dates on it. *Banshee*'s few healthy crewmen made up the funeral procession. Afterward I vowed to visit his grave whenever we returned to port.

"It's a hard thing, dying in a distant place," Tom told me when we returned to the ship. "But George could take comfort, knowing his friends were at hand."

I wasn't convinced. I dreamed that night of my little brother. He would have been seven that summer. I imagined him walking along the shore, waving as I sailed past. He looked so lost and lonely! Then George appeared and took his hand.

A storm blew up during the night, rattling the windows and finally waking me from my dream. I got to my feet and stared at the sheets of rain crashing against the buildings and lashing the ships in the harbor. There was a shrill whine to that wind, and I was reminded of Mother's tales of the banshees, those homeless and vengeful spirits that haunted the coast of my homeland.

"Be at peace, George," I whispered as I stood bare-foot, draped in an oversize nightshirt. "Be at peace, Christopher."

What peace was there to find in Nassau or anywhere else, though?

We were another week getting the rest of the crew well and signing on replacements. To lift our spirits, Robert hosted a party at the governor's house. I didn't want to go, but he insisted. I was in no mood for the rich food and laughing businessmen. Early on I slipped outside and sat alone in the garden. Andrea found me there.

"I'm sorry about your friend," she said, sitting beside me on the iron bench. "There's not a soul in Nassau who hasn't lost someone to yellow fever."

"Probably not," I replied.

I didn't really want to talk about George or anything else. I had spent all morning reading a fresh batch of letters from home and answering each one. I wanted to share my sadness with my family, but I didn't. Mother would only worry more.

"You were lucky," Andrea finally told me. "I've never had a close friend. Not somebody I could really talk to."

"No sisters or brothers?" I asked.

"No one, Henry. George O'Neal may be gone, but you still have your cousin."

"George saved my life," I said, staring at my feet. "He risked his life to do it. Never considered it. I'll never find as good a friend anywhere."

"I'd hate to think I'll never have such a friend," Andrea said, lifting my chin. "We're neither of us ancient, after all. We'll have other friends."

"I wish I could believe you," I told her. "But just now

it seems I've got more enemies than friends. More troubles than a solitary person can carry."

"You could try sharing them."

"It's not that easy, Andrea," I told her. "It hurts even thinking about George. About my father. And I've got work to do."

"That work may get you killed," she warned. "The blockade's tightened. Do you know Captain Bell is due in Nassau any day now? My uncle knows him. He could secure you a place as midshipman. Then we'd no longer be on opposite sides. It's far safer duty too."

"I can't," I told her. "You have to be loyal to your country. I have only my family. That's Robert."

"I heard about *Niphon,* Henry. And the fire. You won't be lucky forever."

"I'm not feeling very lucky just now," I told her.

"Maybe we could dance?"

"You'll have to excuse me," I said, shaking my head. "I just don't have the energy."

"Henry?"

"I'm nobody to worry over," I assured her. "We're on separate paths, Andrea. Leave me to go my way."

"Even if it's the wrong way?"

"Especially if it's the wrong way," I replied. "There's no chart that can tell you what course to steer all the time. Fa told me that when I was only nine. Sometimes you have to work your way through shallow water, past dangerous shoals. That's what I'm doing now. Enjoy the party. Find some better company."

"I wish I knew something to say. Something to comfort you."

"I don't want to be comforted," I told her.

She put her hand on my shoulder as if to keep me there. I lightly eased her fingers away and rose to my feet. Then I walked out the garden gate and headed back to Robert's rooms.

10

BANSHEE CARRIED ALMOST every imaginable cargo during her cruises through the Yank blockade, but none was more bizarre than that which two Confederate officials led aboard the following morning. Some agent in Egypt had sent out a purebred Arabian horse as a gift for the rebel president, Jefferson Davis, and Robert agreed to carry it aboard *Banshee*.

"Insanity," Mr. Erskine grumbled when he spotted the animal. "Insanity!"

To be truthful, I wasn't convinced it was the smartest thing in the world either. You couldn't put a horse down below in the hold, and we had little enough deck as it was. Although we had managed to repair our turtleback, our cabin was little more than a charred cinder. The notion of sleeping on deck with a nervous horse prancing about was none too comforting.

It was too late to discuss the matter, though. The moonless period began that night, and Captain Steele was determined to go to sea. If we wouldn't wait to complete *Banshee*'s repairs, we wouldn't pause to debate taking the Confederate president's horse!

Of all the runs we made through the blockade, none

was more difficult for me than that voyage. Whenever I turned to my duties, I found myself missing George. All the new crewmen hired in Nassau were older, and none of them paid much attention to me. Robert seemed pre-occupied with the cargo, especially that horse. It was as if I had become invisible.

Unfortunately our animal passenger was not. Old Jeff, as we had taken to calling him, left little reminders on deck. I got the special duty of sweeping his deposits into the sea and washing the residue from the deck.

I was also charged with feeding the beast, which was far from easy. He didn't like the oats Jubal prepared and twice nearly bit my fingers off when I tried to hang a feedbag over his ears. John Bailey suggested hanging a hood over the horse's head so he wouldn't be able to see, but nobody could get close enough to try such a tactic.

For two and a half days Old Jeff was the torment of my life. Whenever I was awake, he was making trouble. And twice when I was asleep, he managed to chew through his halter rope and gallop along the deck, nearly trampling me.

"I believe that horse is a Yankee," Tom declared.

"Well, he's sure no sea horse," John added with a cackle.

It was no laughing matter that night. As we were slipping through the Federal blockaders on a quiet night, the fool animal took to neighing.

"He smells the land," Jubal announced. "Give him the feedbag."

I suppose Jubal's idea was that a full mouth made less noise, but Old Jeff wasn't about to cooperate. With me at my lookout post, Jubal had to tie on the feedbag himself.

For a rebel with grandsons in the cavalry, he had no better luck than I did. Old Jeff knocked the feedbag aside and bit Jubal right on the seat of his pants. The cook screamed in pain.

As somebody led Jubal off to recover, Tom Burroughs threw his coat over the wayward steed's head. A blanket followed, and the animal quieted down. We steamed on through the enemy line and cheerfully passed Fort Fisher.

Old Jeff did us a good turn when we arrived in Wilmington. Again the medical inspector assigned us to the quarantine. The whole coast was in a panic over yellow fever.

"Most of the crew has had it," Robert explained.

"Most isn't all," the rebel doctor replied. "Besides, it doesn't mean you can't pass the sickness to others."

"We have vital cargo aboard," Captain Steele complained.

"That horse is a gift for President Davis," Tom added.

"If we're to anchor a week or more, " Robert pointed out, "the horse will have to be destroyed. We have no forage for the animal, and it isn't conducive to our health to have an animal aboard."

That was an understatement!

The rebel doctor walked over and spoke with the two officers who had come with him. They talked for several minutes.

"You can move to the wharf and discharge the horse," the doctor told us. "Then you must return to quarantine."

It didn't exactly work as planned, though. No sooner had we tied up than two of our newest crewmen leaped off the stern and raced on into town. Others followed.

Angry Confederates barked at Captain Steele and Robert, but there was little point in sending us back to the quarantine line. Instead we watched with no little satisfaction as Jeff Davis passed into the hands of other poor wretches. Robert and I prepared our cargo manifests for the harbormaster.

We spent only three days in Wilmington. While slaves unloaded boxes of rifles, kegs of gunpowder, and barrels of pork and beef, Robert set off to locate carpenters to rebuild our deck cabin. With hammers banging away night and day, we sought refuge in a small hotel. Of course, Robert was soon off arranging the purchase of cotton. I was alone.

For a boy raised with brothers and accustomed to work, idleness was the worst sort of curse. Within an hour I was going crazy. I finally left the hotel and made my way along the shops and gaming houses that lay between the hotel and the docks. Every red-haired boy reminded me of George. I had never felt so alone.

"I suppose your ship's back," a smallish boy called from the other side of a market stall.

"Pardon?" I asked.

"You don't remember me," he said, frowning. "You gave my cousin Marty and me some bread. Last spring."

I nodded. "You're named Francis, like my brother."

"That's right," he said. "It was good bread. You must have a good cook."

"He fell overboard," I told him.

"And your friend, the one with the red hair?"

"Yellow fever."

"My cousin's joined the army, but they wouldn't take me. Too sickly, they say. But I haven't seen many soldiers who look any healthier."

"Probably not," I agreed. "You're selling peaches now?"

"Today. Tomorrow I'll be shining shoes. Maybe running telegraph messages. 'Frank,' somebody will say, 'we've got some work you can do.' Nobody pays much, but I feed myself."

"Don't you have any family?" Francis shook his head. "Anywhere?" I asked. He shook his head again. "Ever been to sea?" I asked.

"Only in a boat on the river," he answered.

"Stop by *Banshee*," I urged. "I have a feeling we may need a man or two for the trip back to Nassau."

By the time the carpenters finished and our cargo was aboard, Francis had signed on as second ship's boy. He was half a head shorter and a year younger than I was, but rough living had made him a hardy sort. He was sure to be a good companion. He had a far better voice for singing than I did, and he played a banjo even better. We all were glad of his company, especially me.

With our cabin repaired and the hull covered with a fresh coat of gray paint, I looked forward to a more comfortable voyage. I was quickly disappointed.

"Henry, come over here," Robert called.

I hurried to his side, but I didn't spot his usual grin. Two men stood beside him.

"These gentlemen will sail with us to Nassau," Robert explained. "Unfortunately they will need our cabin."

"The *whole* cabin?" I asked.

"Henry, they're important men," Robert whispered. "Besides, you won't have a horse trampling you this time."

"No, just a thousand bales of cotton squeezing every inch of space."

"Well, I'll earn a thousand dollars this trip, and I'll be sleeping on a blanket right next to you."

He gripped my shoulders, and I couldn't help cracking a smile. "I guess it won't be so bad," I told him.

"You can invite Francis to join us," he said, nodding toward the bow where Francis was strumming his banjo.

"Hope he doesn't snore," I said.

"George did, and it never bothered you."

"You couldn't even notice when the engines were running," I pointed out. "Besides, George was never any real trouble."

"You miss him, do you?"

"Most days," I confessed. "I miss Fa too. And Mother. Colleen, Tim, and Francis too. I'm good at missing people."

"We'll try not to lose anybody else," Robert promised.

"Yes, let's do," I agreed.

11

CAPTAIN STEELE GUIDED us skillfully through the Yankees that night. We didn't even hear a lookout shouting at us. Twice we were within a hundred yards of a warship, but each time we slipped past unnoticed.

I stayed on watch until first light. One of the new-comers, a fellow named King, took my place. He was from Baltimore and had been stranded in Nassau when his ship sailed without him. He was a capable sailor, but I didn't particularly like him. He was one of the men who had jumped onto the wharf and broken quarantine. He told Francis the first good breeze would probably sweep both of us into the Atlantic.

King wasn't much of a lookout either. I had just nod-ded off to sleep when Mr. Erskine's voice woke me.

"Smoke!" he shouted. "Look astern there!"

I shook myself conscious and stared in disbelief. No more than four miles behind us sailed a large side-wheel cruiser with three masts. She had every inch of canvas set, steam up, and was coming on fast.

"Unbelievable," Robert grumbled as he crawled out of our cotton nest and headed forward. "Where are the lookouts?"

The only thing that saved us from destruction or capture was the chance arrival of Mr. Erskine on deck. He had left the engines to get a little fresh air. Otherwise the Yanks would have had us with scarcely a finger's worth of effort.

"Henry, scramble up there and tell that no-account King to get down here," Tom said. "I'll show him how a Carolinian rewards a man who's sleeping on duty."

"He's just off watch," John Bailey said, waving me back to my makeshift bed. "Leave it to me."

Now Bailey wasn't but five and a half feet tall, and even after a full meal he didn't weigh a hundred twenty pounds. King was a big fellow, over six feet, and maybe twice Bailey's girth. Wee John, as he liked to be called, was up the mast fast as lightning, though, and King came scurrying down almost as fast. He wasn't asleep, but I could smell the whiskey ten feet away.

Tom planted a boot on King's rump and kicked him to the deck. The hands cheered, but there wasn't really time to punish a drunk. We had more pressing concerns, mainly a Yank cruiser on our heels.

I'd been to sea only a few months, but even I could tell that with a freshening breeze and steam to help, the Yanks were bound to catch us. Mr. Erskine coaxed every ounce of speed from *Banshee,* but our engines had never provided the promised power. I went forward to see if I could help Robert, but in truth only speed would save us now.

"This will never do," Captain Steele announced as he barked out a new course. *Banshee* swung away from Nassau and headed directly into the wind.

It was a clever trick. The Yanks had been so close that

I could see the faces of the officers gathered on their bow. Our new course caught them off guard and gave us the chance to regain our lead. Moreover, they had to take in their sails, as the stiffening breeze was little help to them now.

Using his eyeglass, the captain identified our stalker as *James Adger*. Robert found it on the navy lists.

"Eight 32-pounders," he announced. "She'll have to close the distance."

"Yes, but they're doing just that," Captain Steele said, motioning toward the enemy ship.

I could tell that everyone expected capture. Robert went so far as to fetch his money belt from its hiding place under his sea chest in our cabin. He had sixty gold sovereigns in that belt, and he parceled them out among the officers so that they would have some money should the Yanks seize us. He gave me two pounds.

"They may take me somewhere else," he said, gazing seriously into my eyes. "Hide the money. Use it sparingly."

As *James Adger* closed the distance, we grew more desperate. The captain and Robert conferred for a moment. Then Robert shouted to begin loosening the ropes securing our deck cargo. "Toss it off the stern," he urged. "You don't want to damage the paddle floats."

I could see the pain on his face. Each of those bales represented fifty or sixty pounds' profit in Liverpool. For once I was glad I was no longer an investor in deck cargo.

One at a time we rolled those bales off the stern. It was odd, gazing back at the bobbing bales. They resembled sugar cubes floating in a cup of boiling tea. It must have been a temptation for the Yanks, seeing thousands of dollars drifting by, but they never even slowed. Once we had shed the extra weight, though, *Banshee*'s engines roared anew. We picked up speed and began to pull away.

"To think of it," Robert lamented. "Ten bales of Sea Island cotton. Eight hundred pounds easy."

As we continued to clear the deck cargo, Francis shouted in alarm. Between two bales, in a hole formed by hemp bags, was a black man. He rose slowly and eyed us warily.

"He's a slave," Francis said, pointing to the man's rough clothes.

"Not anymore," Captain Steele declared. "Aboard the Queen's ship, he's a free man."

The slave, who announced his name was Jacob, thanked the captain and then joined in the task of hurling cotton overboard.

"At least we've made one man happy," Robert remarked.

When we next arrived in Wilmington, the story of our runaway got out. Robert had to pay the man's master four thousand Confederate dollars.

What amazed me was that I had been sleeping no more than three feet from Jacob. Engines could conceal more than snoring, I decided.

For a time it appeared that we would leave our dogged pursuer behind. *Banshee*'s engines again let us down, though. The sea was growing heavy, and the bearings became overheated. An exasperated Mr. Erskine appeared on deck to explain we would have to reduce speed.

"And be taken?" Captain Steele asked.

"We're cooking those bearings, Captain," the engineer explained. "I've no way of cooling them."

"There's a way," old Jubal said, grinning. "I remember from my days on the Mississippi River. You mix yourself a little oil and sulfur. It works as a good lubricant."

"And you have both at hand, I suppose?" Mr. Erskine asked.

"Salad oil will do," Jubal explained. "Put in a little gunpowder."

Our cook saved our hides with his odd concoction. I myself worried we might blow ourselves to high heaven, putting gunpowder onto hot bearings, but the oil apparently removed the explosive quality of the powder. At any rate we regained our lead and added to it. Toward nightfall we were nearly five miles ahead. *James Adger* finally turned away. We cheered.

We had dodged the Yankee cruiser for fifteen hours. We were a hundred fifty miles off course. Captain Steele headed us south, toward Bermuda. We were sure to run short of coal, and he hoped to replenish our supplies and then continue along to Nassau.

In my relief to see the Yankees gone, I failed to appreciate the perils that remained. We had burned our best coal, and even after reducing speed, we were sure to empty our bunkers before long. We had lost a day steaming north and east, so we were another day recovering the distance. By then the coal was nearly gone. We were forced to chop down our mainmast, tear apart our new deck cabin, and finally begin burning cotton and turpentine from the hold. We were making less than three knots when we finally sighted land. We anchored near the northeast keys of Bermuda.

Our saga was far from over, though. There was no coal to be had in the little harbor town, and the best Robert could do was arrange a schooner to carry him south to secure coal in Nassau. Meanwhile a new Yank cruiser appeared on the horizon.

"We're finished," Francis said when he spotted the vessel.

"No, we're safe here," I explained. "They won't dare disturb a British ship in British waters."

"Won't keep them from blocking our escape to Nassau," Tom pointed out.

The Yank ship circled just outside the territorial limit for three entire days, but Robert was a week arranging the coal. The Yanks displayed a fair measure of patience, but they couldn't stay forever. The fourth morning we noticed they were gone.

It was just as well, for *Banshee* was in a sorry state. Stripped of every scrap of wood above decks, with only the foremast still standing, she looked little better than she had after the fire. By the time Robert returned in the schooner, we had resorted to eating cold biscuits and sorghum. Our other provisions were long gone.

I passed the week in Bermuda with either Francis or Jacob, the escaped slave. Being the only ship's boys, Francis and I were rarely assigned the same watch, so most of my waking hours I passed with Jacob. I had a thousand questions for him, but he was a quiet sort who only rarely spoke. When he did, it was usually worth listening.

"A slave never knows a sunny day," he told me. "There's always a cloud of misery up there, choking the life out of you."

Although I could never know what it was like to be a slave, I could read the misery etched on Jacob's face. It wasn't because of the work. Jacob cheerfully helped shift cargo in the holds, and he even lent Jubal a hand in the galley.

"I don't understand why you would dig yourself a hole like that," I said as we ate our biscuits that last day in Bermuda. "If we hadn't thrown the cotton overboard, you might have starved. Or smothered."

"Dying's not the worst thing that can happen to a man," he replied.

"What is?" I asked.

"Being alone," he said, sighing. "Seeing the people you love sent away, sold to somebody you never heard of. A slave never has any say over what he does, what he wears, what he eats, if he sleeps. He's no better than a dog. Truth is, I've known dogs treated a lot better."

"What will you do in Nassau, Jacob?"

"Find myself a life," he said, smiling broadly. "For that I'll have you men to thank."

I guess the most surprising thing about Jacob was how well he got along with Francis and Jubal. I'd always heard southerners didn't associate with slaves. Jubal welcomed his help and even praised his talent for stretching a bit of flour and baking powder farther than anyone he'd ever met. As for Francis, he laughed when I asked about Jacob. "I never owned any slaves, but I've been close to one myself," he told me.

"You mean, working hard?"

"I think you know exactly what I mean," he said. "Being by yourself. Knowing any day you could be kicked about, starved, beaten. I hear you thrashing around in your sleep sometimes, talking about this or that."

"What?"

"Who's Christopher?"

I frowned. As I spoke of the little brother I'd never even had a chance to know, I felt Francis grip my hand.

"I had a brother die too," he said. "At Bull Run, in the war. He was sixteen. A Yankee cannonball just took his head right off his shoulders. When we got the news, Ma shriveled up and died. Pa joined the army and got himself killed at Fredericksburg."

"Were these battles?" I asked.

"Battles. Places. I never even heard of them before the war. There's nothing left of my family but me. Like Jacob. Like you."

"No, I've got a mother, a sister, and two brothers back in Liverpool," I said. "And my cousin Robert aboard *Banshee*."

"Then why do you always seem so alone?" he asked.

I had no answer for him.

12

AFTER OUR SEPTEMBER encounter with *James Adger*, half the crew left *Banshee*. Our close brush with death or capture, followed by the long week stranded in Bermuda, left us all weary. Several of the stokers chose work above decks on other ships. Captain Steele dismissed three of the new crewmen, including King, for failing to do their duty.

As replacements Robert hired a dozen men off a Canadian schooner. The others came to us from Liverpool aboard a merchantman.

Our next two runs were as uneventful as they were successful. By November Williams Brothers had purchased a handful of blockade-runners, most of them faster and better built than *Banshee*. The new *Will-of-the-Wisp* was the best of the lot. Her arrival brought me to a moment of decision.

"Henry, what did your mother say this time?" Robert asked when I finished reading my latest stack of letters.

"The same old thing," I answered. "She wants me to come home."

"Maybe it's time," he said. "Henry, I'm leaving *Banshee*. From now on I'll be supercargo aboard *Will-of-the-Wisp*."

"And me?"

"That ship has a full crew, Henry. I asked, but they don't need another boy, even a sharp-eyed one. You know, *Banshee* has earned me a lot of money. You've done fairly well yourself. You could return to Liverpool and go to school. Mr. Williams would provide you a place in the business."

"It's too late," I said, staring out toward the harbor. "The sea's in my blood. I'm no different from Fa."

"Maybe not, but the blockade is tightening. They caught ten ships the past two weeks. Henry, you can sail from Nassau to Liverpool. See your family. A sailor can always find a ship sailing somewhere in Liverpool."

"But you're not quitting."

"I have a job to do."

"Don't I?" I asked.

I had my answer to that question soon enough. Captain Steele dropped by with a bottle of brandy to congratulate Robert on his new assignment. As they drank and talked, the captain called me in from the next room. "So, will you go back to England now, Henry?" he asked.

"Do I have a choice?" I asked.

"As long as I have a ship under my feet, you'll have a place aboard her," he assured me. "I've come here to offer you a berth and a raise, with your cousin's approval. Sixty pounds salary. That's more than an admiral makes. Of course, you have better eyesight."

"I'm younger too," I said, cracking a smile.

"We need you, Henry," the captain said, drawing me to his side. "You're our good-luck charm."

"If so, I didn't do George or Bob Jones much good."

"The sea's not without its hazards, as you know. Still, I want you badly. That little rebel snipe Frank never quits jabbering. I need someone to keep him busy."

So I stayed on *Banshee*. It felt odd to sail without Robert. Even though his duties had taken more and more of his time, I had always felt safe in his company. Now he was off on his new ship, and I was more alone than I imagined possible.

I slung a hammock below, with the rest of the crew, for it was too cold and wet to sleep on deck in November. Before, I had been spared the heavier work of stowing cargo, but now that I was paid a seaman's wage, I joined in. Frank, as Francis had started calling himself, shared every idle moment with me. I found myself teaching him the same hitches and knots that George had taught me not half a year earlier. We couldn't talk of Ireland, but we could sing and dream and talk of the pretty girls we'd see when we reached Wilmington.

We set out in mid-November with a particularly vital cargo. We carried enough coffee, soap, and food to keep Robert E. Lee's Army of Northern Virginia on the battle-field a whole month. We also carried cases of new rifles and sorely needed shoes. *Banshee*'s successes made her a marked ship, and I couldn't help but notice Andrea Fornier and her uncle studying us from across the harbor. A Yank cruiser had left two days before, and we were likely to see her once we cleared land.

Captain Steele was unmatched as a captain at sea, though, and he lost the cruiser by steaming into a squall. The second day out of Nassau we spied two other blockade-runners, but we encountered no enemy ship. That night I stood watch at my station on the foremast, keeping my eyes peeled for trouble. Frank brought me a cup of hot tea a little after midnight. "You should have a blanket," he told me. "It's freezing up here."

"You don't want to get too comfortable," I said, sipping my tea. "You have to stay alert."

The following night we started our run into Wilmington. Robert had been right about the blockade. There were even more cruisers and gunboats lurking about. Tom chose to swing farther north than ever. Perhaps that was our undoing. The Carolina coast was full of treacherous stretches, and we had to stand back to sea twice when fog obscured the shoreline. The first traces of dawn had painted the eastern sky as we finally approached the mouth of the Cape Fear River.

"Lord help us," Tom called as the line of blockading ships appeared on the brightening horizon.

"Keep a keen eye out for trouble, Henry!" Captain Steele shouted.

"Trouble?" Tom cried. "The whole Yankee fleet's in front of us!"

Our sole chance of reaching Wilmington was to surprise the enemy by pure audacity. The Yanks could scarcely expect us to run past them in daylight. And if our luck deserted us, we could at least look forward to an exciting duel with one of the new swift steamers.

It was not to be.

The first Union vessel to give chase was *Fulton,* an army transport. *Fulton* was not even part of the blockade. She was sailing along the coast carrying soldiers. The ship was armed, though, and after a chase of better than an hour she opened up on us with a big rifled gun.

The first shot fell short, and Mr. Erskine ordered

more steam. The Yanks adjusted their fire, however, and *Fulton's* big gun sent a second shell into our bow. The third shot holed us aft, and the stokers poured onto the deck, complaining that we were sunk for certain.

We were taking water, but there was no fire or danger of sinking. Nevertheless, Captain Steele announced that the jig was up. "Come about!" he shouted.

As *Banshee* began a slow turn, a Yankee warship appeared from the opposite direction. The newcomer fired four times, sending shells crashing into the sea just ahead. Pinned in and crippled, we had no choice but surrender.

I remained at my post atop the foremast for almost ten minutes. It was as if I imagined that I could avoid the awful reality of capture by staying aloft. Frank climbed up to get me, though, and together we lined up and awaited the boatful of Yankees approaching our port bow.

"Be brave, boys," Captain Steele urged. "They're sailors themselves, and they won't harm you. We're unarmed and will offer no resistance."

I couldn't help feeling low. Tom hung his head and eyed the distant coast. It was much too far to swim. Otherwise he might have chanced it.

Captain Steele, who had been a prisoner before, tried to remain calm. I could tell he was sick to be handing over our ship to the enemy, though.

I made my way toward John Bailey and Keith Davis, both members of the original crew who had survived cannonballs, fire, and disease.

"Good luck to you, Henry," Wee John said.

"Practice those knots, boy," Keith added. "You'll make a sailor yet."

I shook their hands and returned to Frank. He too stared longingly at the coast. He had known happiness there once.

"Here, take this," Captain Steele said, handing me a smallish gold coin. It was twenty United States dollars. "It may buy you better treatment."

The captain meted out a coin to every man of the crew. He needn't have bothered. The boarders were soldiers, not sailors. They belonged to the First Rhode Island Cavalry. The first thing they did was search us, and they pocketed everything of value. They even took my small silver cross.

A Lieutenant Darling was in charge, and he sent three men forward to seize our charts. Another man went below to check our cargo.

"The war's over for you men," the lieutenant declared. "You'll be in New York before the week's gone."

EPILOGUE

AT FIRST BEING a prisoner of war wasn't so bad. We were taken aboard a dispatch ship and kept together, apart from the officers, on deck. The food was decent, and our guards often recounted their own adventures chasing steamers along the coast or at sea. All that changed when we entered New York Harbor.

To begin with, it was already late November, and the weather was foggy and cold. I had always imagined arriving in New York as so many Irish boys had, ready to begin a great new adventure in America. Instead the adventure was over, and I arrived to face an uncertain future.

Our new home was Fort Lafayette, part of the city's harbor defenses. The officers were taken away to a city jail, and we were split among several damp dark cells in the fort's interior. Frank and I found ourselves sharing a large cavernlike room with a mixed assortment of Irish, English, and southern sailors, most of them ten years or more older. Except for a brief visit from the British ambassador, who didn't promise to make much effort on behalf of a fatherless Irish boy, we were left to ourselves. The food consisted of bowls of corn mush with a few chunks of bacon. After a week Frank and I were pale, thin, and totally discouraged.

That was when Meara O'Shea appeared.

I was sitting on a ragged blanket in one corner of the cell with Frank when two tall, stern-faced soldiers arrived with muskets in hand. "Severn," one of them called. "Come along."

Frank and I exchanged uneasy looks, but when the second soldier unlocked the cell's iron gate, I stood up and joined the soldiers.

"Cheer up, boy," the first man said. "You've got a visitor."

"A what?" I asked.

"We're taking you to the commandant's office," the second man said, laughing. "Not to the gallows."

A hundred thoughts raced through my brain. Had Captain Steele come to free me? Was the British ambassador waiting? Instead I was presented to a smiling woman of thirty-five years dressed in a modest yellow cotton dress.

"Oh, my dear boy!" she exclaimed as she embraced me. "You have your dear father's eyes. Captain, you can't keep a mere child in a place like this! Do you hear?"

I stared at the strange, fiery-eyed, red-haired woman in disbelief as she marched around the office, bullying the young captain. She seemed like a guardian angel sent to rescue me from the pits of despair. After pointing out that her brother was a colonel in the army currently besieging Richmond, Virginia, she turned back to me.

"Well, Henry, what have you to say for yourself?" she asked.

"Ma'am?" I gasped.

"You don't wish to stay here, do you?"

"No," I admitted. "Can you get me released? Are you from the British Ambassador's office?"

"I am not!" she barked. "Don't you recognize your own blood, Henry Severn? I'm your aunt Meara!"

"Mother's sister," I said, studying her. "But how—"

"You do remember writing your mother?" Aunt Meara asked.

I nodded. No letter had ever been more difficult to compose.

"Adara's never been one to waste time," Aunt Meara explained. "She sent word to me immediately. Still, a ship takes a few days to cross an ocean."

"And you're going to help?" I asked.

"That's mostly up to you, son," the captain said, producing a long sheet of paper.

"We've got some bargaining to do," Aunt Meara whispered. "The captain has enough sailors to feed. What he needs are crewmen for the navy. You, on the other hand, would like to be free of this place. Am I right?" I nodded. "Your father found life at sea a worthy profession. Perhaps you will find it the same."

"You want me to join the Union navy?" I asked.

"It's a simple enough choice," the captain announced. "It's the only way out of here. There's fresh air and honest work. What's more, I'm authorized to return your captured possessions, including this." He produced Captain Steele's gold piece.

"If the navy's not to your liking, your uncle Patrick commands a regiment in Virginia," Aunt Meara added. "My own oldest boy, your cousin Tom, serves there."

All this was news to me. Mother had talked often of

the sisters and brother who had gone to America, but I had heard nothing of them since leaving Liverpool.

"I'd be more use at sea," I said. "I'm not the best sailor alive, but I have sharp eyes and a willingness to learn."

"It's the navy then," the captain said, handing me the enlistment paper. I read the words and then signed. Because I was less than eighteen years of age, Aunt Meara also signed, acting as my guardian.

"He's to report to the navy yard next week," the captain told Aunt Meara. "He'll get his orders there."

"Thank you, Captain," she replied. "Come along now, Henry."

I paused for a moment. "There's someone I must tell good-bye," I said. "Is it possible to return to the cells for a few minutes?"

"You won't be welcomed there," the captain told me. "Those men are your enemies now."

I sighed. Still, I couldn't just walk away without saying anything to Frank.

The soldiers escorted me back to the cells. Instead of allowing me to enter, though, they permitted Frank to step out into the corridor.

"You're leaving," he announced before I had a chance to explain. "Some of the others said you probably would. Signed on with the Yankees, I suppose."

"My aunt came to visit," I explained. "I have an uncle and a cousin in the Yankee army."

"Well, that's more family than I have anywhere," he said, sighing.

"You angry with me, Frank?" I asked.

"Why would I be?" he asked, shaking his head. "They

don't improve the food, I'll probably sign on myself before long. If they get desperate enough for sailors, they might even take me."

I tried to laugh, but it wasn't possible. There was an odor of despair in the cells, and I found nothing humorous about little Frank remaining there.

"I'll send some food," I promised. "And a blanket."

"Sure," Frank said, nodding. "I appreciate that."

"I'll ask my aunt to visit. Maybe she can argue you out of here too."

"Maybe so."

The soldiers announced it was time to leave, and I turned to go. Frank gave me a farewell nod and then returned to the cell. As I marched down the corridor with the soldiers, I said farewell to Wee John, Keith, and several other old friends from *Banshee*. It didn't seem entirely fair, my going free while Frank and the others remained behind. But then life was rarely fair.

I met Aunt Meara outside the commandant's office. She led the way toward the fort's main gate. As we walked, she told me of the five cousins awaiting my arrival at the house her husband, Michael, had built over his carpentry shop. She promised to show me all the wonders of the largest city in America. Already I could see lines of ships coming and going in the harbor.

"It's a grand place, Henry," she told me. "A young man can build himself a future here."

"Yes," I agreed. I thought of the days to come and the ship I would join. Perhaps fresh adventures and new friends lay ahead. But I knew I would never find better friends or greater adventures than I had known aboard *Banshee* during our days together running the blockade.

Author's Note

Although there was no Henry Severn, much of this story is true. Thomas Taylor, who served as *Banshee*'s supercargo and is the model for Robert Severn, recounted his adventures in *Running the Blockade: A Personal Narrative of Adventures, Risks, and Escapes During the American Civil War*. This remarkable book first appeared in 1896 and is considered a nautical classic.

Much of the technical information, as well as descriptions of *Banshee*'s encounters with Federal vessels, comes from *Official Records of the Union and Confederate Navies in the War of the Rebellion* and its companion volumes, *The War of the Rebellion: A Compilation of the Official Records of the Union and Confederate Armies*. There are a number of original accounts written by officers of blockading ships and by men who ran the blockade to other ports, including the Gulf ports of my home state of Texas. I chose to write about *Banshee* because she was unusually successful and because Wilmington was the most important of the southern ports from the summer of 1862 onward.

On November 20, 1863, *Banshee*'s career as a blockade-runner came to an end. The steamer arrived in New York and was condemned by a prize court. The United States Navy paid $72,500 for the vessel on March 12, 1864, and she served on the Atlantic blockade the last thirteen months of the war.

Except for Captain Steele, whose release was secured by the British ambassador, most of *Banshee*'s crew spent eight months as prisoners at Fort Lafayette in New York Harbor. Conditions were poor, and the food was worse. The fort's commander complained that he lacked the supplies to provide for his prisoners. Eventually the British sailors returned home or enlisted in the growing United States Navy.

Blockade-runners continued to penetrate the line of Federal ships around Wilmington and Charleston until the war's final year. When Fort Fisher fell on January 15, 1865, Wilmington was effectively closed as a port. The city itself held out until February, when Confederate General Braxton Bragg evacuated his soldiers and left Union soldiers to occupy a virtually deserted Wilmington.

Banshee was replaced by a better steamer of the same name, commanded by the freed Captain Steele. *Banshee II* continued to penetrate the blockade until the last of the Atlantic ports fell.

It's not accidental that I chose an Irish boy to tell this story. My own great-great-grandfather Bernard McCormick sailed to the United States from Liverpool in 1850. He proudly wore the uniform of his adopted nation while serving in the Tenth Illinois Cavalry Regiment. Most of my mother's family also came to the United States from Ireland.

I would like to acknowledge the research assistance of the staff at the United States Military History Institute at Carlisle Barracks, Pennsylvania; the Center for American History at the University of Texas at Austin; and the United States National Archives and Records Administration. I also appreciate the use of facilities at the University of Texas at Dallas, the University of North Texas, and the main branch of the Dallas Public Library, repository for the Dallas Genealogical Society's extensive collections.